Martin a [barcode obscures text] **of
them tha**

He rem[oved his] glove and, leaning over the saddle, took her hand. His palm was warm and surprisingly uncalloused, but his strength flowed over her, leaving her renewed through its force. She ran the tip of her tongue over her dry lips, then dared to raise her eyes to his.

"You should never wear any color but blue. Turns your eyes to sapphires." His low voice scattered her thoughts like rose petals in the wind. She stood dumb, her hand still resting in his, caught in the trance he induced so expertly. "I'll be back this evening to look in on our friend in the bunkhouse and chop you some wood."

She swallowed and hoped her voice wouldn't reveal the disquiet inside. "That's very kind of you, but I can attend to the poor man when he awakens, and Mr. Hornbeck has offered to stop by. I've put you to enough trouble for one day."

Martin's grip loosened, and he dropped her hand most unceremoniously.

MOON FOR A CANDLE

Maryn Langer

Serenade/Saga
BOOKS

of the Zondervan Publishing House
Grand Rapids, Michigan

A Note From The Author:
I love to hear from my readers! You may correspond with me by writing:

> Maryn Langer
> 1415 Lake Drive, S.E.
> Grand Rapids, MI 49506

MOON FOR A CANDLE
Copyright © 1985 by The Zondervan Corporation
Grand Rapids, Michigan

Serenade Saga is an imprint of Zondervan Publishing House,
1415 Lake Drive, S.E., Grand Rapids, Michigan 49506.

Library of Congress Cataloging in Publication Data

ISBN 0-310-47052-8

All Scripture quotations, unless otherwise noted, are taken from the
HOLY BIBLE: NEW INTERNATIONAL VERSION (North
American Edition). Copyright © 1973, 1978, 1984, by the Interna-
tional Bible Society. Used by permission of Zondervan Bible
Publishers.

Edited by Pamela M. Jewell
Designed by Kim Koning

Printed in the United States of America

85 86 87 88 89 90 / 10 9 8 7 6 5 4 3 2 1

to Kathleen Brown and Terry Montague

CHAPTER 1

1892

ALEXA SPENCE STOOD ON THE COVERED PORCH of the two-story Victorian house—stood staring at the slender brass key lying in the palm of her black leather-gloved hand. The key looked well-used and that seemed strange to her. Back in southern Illinois folks seldom ever locked their doors. What was so different about northern Idaho that houses should always be locked when one left home? A slight shiver of apprehension prickled through her and, for a moment, she considered not unlocking the door. Maybe she should climb back in the buckboard, return to Rathdrum, and take the train back to Mt. Vernon. Maybe she should go on being a telegraph operator and living with Aunt Cassy.

No! Most definitely not! Her bachelor uncle, Clyde Grant, had left her his ranch, and she was going to claim it. With a tenuous motion, she reached out and fitted the key into the lock. A little click told her the lock had found its resting place. She withdrew the key and dropped it into her purse.

Drawing a deep breath in an attempt to calm her heart, she gripped the carved brass doorknob and slowly turned it. The varnished pine door with its window of stained glass swung open on well-oiled hinges. A slight musty smell from a house shut up for several months greeted her as she stepped from the bright sunshine of an early June morning into the dim entrance hall.

She stopped and waited for her eyes to adjust before moving further into the unfamiliar rooms. Why did she have a feeling that someone was watching her? Deep inside the house, boards creaked and Alexa, muscles tensed, jumped at the unexpected sound. Standing at the entrance, but leaving the front door ajar, she slowly removed her gloves.

There it was again! Did empty houses squeak and groan of themselves? In her twenty-three years, she couldn't remember ever having been in a house alone. Aunt Cassy had eight children of her own and five strays like Alexa whom she took in as she would kittens to feed and tend. The loving woman couldn't turn away homeless children or animals and, as a result, her Illinois farm resembled a combination of orphanage and zoo.

But Mt. Vernon was no longer home. Now Alexa possessed her own place— a ranch in northern Idaho. It was time she stopped letting her imagination run wild and explore her new residence.

Alexa had a choice of two doors leading off the entrance hall. Deciding on the one to her left, she carefully opened the door. Again the musty smell assailed her nostrils. At last satisfied that she could breathe comfortably, she crossed the pale gray carpet, patterned with bunches of roses and green leaves, and pulled up the window shades. Sunlight diffused by white lace curtains streamed in to the room. Alexa trailed her fingers along the leaf-green silk brocade and noted with approval the lambrequins that hung

8

from gold cornices. This obviously was the parlor, its sheeted furniture standing protected against the dust, like deformed ghosts.

She examined the crystal chandelier fitted with coal oil lamps hanging in the center of the room. Its faceted prisms and chimneys, dulled by dust and smoke, remained lifeless even in the sunlight.

Passing a large rectangular looking glass in a gold leaf frame that hung lengthwise on the white painted wall. She paused and examined her reflection. "I suppose I could take off my hat since I'm planning to stay."

Raising her arms, she started to remove the hat pins. When the reflection of a definite movement of the draperies behind her caught her eye. She whirled about, hands still suspended.

"Who . . . who's there?" she stammered, fright turning her tongue to wood.

The only answer was a squeaking board on the stairs going to the second floor from the front entrance hall. Alexa unconsciously wiped sweaty palms on her Melton cloth cloak as she looked about the room for a weapon. Spying a poker among the fire tools standing next to the little Lady Franklin stove, she dashed across the parlor, grabbed it and ran into the hall, brandishing the black, hooked iron piece over her head like a sword. She was stopped short in her charge up the stairs, however, by a gangly adolescent cat that managed to get tangled in her flying skirts.

"Meeeooow!" the light gray-and-white animal screeched. It jerked itself free and pranced sideways. Back arched, with tail stiff and straight in the air, it continued to hiss.

Collapsing onto the stairs in relief, Alexa laughed. "So you're the villain who invaded my house and scared me witless. Well, you're very welcome if you'll be a nice kitty and stay out of the curtains." She reached out a hand and curiosity overcame the little

9

beast. "Come here and let's get acquainted." It came
to sniff and she scooped it up into her lap.

After a thorough scratching around the ears and
under the chin, the cat was convinced that Alexa
meant no harm and curled into her lap to take full
advantage of the warming sun.

"You need a name," Alexa said. "I think Tiger's
appropriate even though you're the wrong color. It fits
your nature. Now, down with you. I have more house
to explore now that I know you're the cause for my
mysterious noises."

She dumped Tiger on the floor, retrieved the poker,
and placed it back in its stand. Opening the door next
to the mirror, she entered the dining room.

The long table, covered with an elegant lace cloth
and the eight chairs set around it occupied much of
the room. "My goodness, Tiger, it looks like I shall be
expected to entertain. And in a grand style, too, from
the looks of the china and crystal in the cupboards."
Small shivers of anticipation ran down her spine as
she thought of her new life. Bless Aunt Cassy. She
had trained Alexa well, always insisting on the
observance of proper etiquette and the best china and
linen for the elaborate Sunday dinners she served
each week.

Next, Alexa, with Tiger continually rubbing against
her skirts, found the big kitchen. It had a galvanized
steel sink with a pitcher-spout water pump. Did the
pump actually draw water or was it just a decoration?
She gave the handle a couple of pumps, but nothing
happened. If it did provide water directly into the
kitchen, it had lost its prime from disuse. No matter.
There was time enough later to find out. The walls
were lined with tall cupboards reaching from floor to
ceiling, packed with all manner of cooking utensils. A
great range handsomely ornamented with nickel trim
and sculptured iron stood against the outside wall. It
had both a high warming closet over the six hole stove

and low warming closet under the oven. The oversized water reservoir on the side was mounted with brass couplings. A full woodbox was placed conveniently next to it.

"What a lovely kitchen! I have arrived in paradise," she said, and clapped her hands with the joy of it. But if it was paradise, she was sharing it, for again she had the feeling of being watched.

She hurried out into the hall and entered a room behind the kitchen. The sitting room, convenient and private, was decorated with walls painted a soft green. Pushing aside the lace Nottingham curtains, she opened the windows to provide some cross ventilation.

"The sooner we get this place aired out, the better," she said to Tiger.

Alexa walked to the corner where a tall, black, nickel-ornamented heating stove stood. In the ceiling above the stove, a register had been cut that allowed the heat to rise and warm the room above. She crossed the room and looked up into the register. A shadow moved. She was sure of it. The hair on the back of her neck stood up, and her heart surged into her throat. Another creak! She froze and managed not to cry out only by exerting the greatest control.

Trembling knees barely carried her to the nearest chair, and she collapsed into it. Tiger leaped into her lap and she sat, absent-mindedly petting him, while she tried to recover her composure. "What are we going to do?" she spoke softly to the cat. "There isn't anyone around for miles who can help us." She looked about the room and noticed a cabinet in which rested a wide variety of guns. "There's a veritable arsenal, but I've never fired a weapon in my life." Alexa hugged the cat to her. "Oh, Tiger, I'm so frightened."

Another creak from overhead! A small involuntary cry escaped. Never in her memory had she faced a crisis alone. And she felt defenseless.

11

Slowly rising, she made her way to the gun cabinet. Selecting one of the smaller rifles. She took it from the cabinet and placed it to her shoulder as she had seen Aunt Cassy's boys do. If she could find some ammunition, she might even be able to load and shoot it. Then, she stopped her rummaging. Did she really think she could shoot someone? She, who cried all the time she was skinning the wild birds the boys brought home for roasting?

She started to return the gun to its resting place in the cabinet. *Now, wait a minute. Whoever is in this house doesn't know anything about me. I could be a regular Calamity Jane for all he knows.* Alexa laid the gun on the table and removed her hat. She draped her cape over a chair and knelt to pray. "Dear Lord, I can't remember when I've needed You more. I ask You to be with me so I won't do something foolish. Please don't let anyone hurt me—and don't let *me* hurt anyone in panic. Give me courage. I'm in great need of courage. I'm scared—so scared. Worse than ever before in my life." Alexa continued to kneel, trying to quiet her racing heart and collect her wits. Finally, she felt a calmness flow through her. "Thank you, Lord. Amen."

Standing, she nervously picked up the gun and cradling it in her arm, marched into the hall and up the stairs.

The first door at the top of the stairs opened into a lovely bedroom. Alexa could quickly see, even in the dim light coming through the window shade, that the room was empty. Unless someone was hiding in the wardrobe. She didn't intend to open it to find out.

"Come on, Tiger," she called softly as she stepped back into the hall, closing the door behind her.

The door into the next bedroom stood ajar. Raising the empty gun to her shoulder, she kicked the door open with her foot, stepped through the doorway, and pointed the gun into the empty bedroom. Whoever had been there earlier had slipped away.

"Do you suppose he went downstairs and out the open front door?" she asked the cat. Satisfied that that was indeed the case, Alexa lowered the gun and stepped back into the hall.

From the second floor, the stairway turned into a spiral leading to the attic. "I guess we can leave the attic for a bit later," she said, but Tiger disagreed. He bounded up the stairs and stood clawing on the door.

"Very well, if you insist."

This door didn't open easily as the others had, but by pushing with her shoulder, she forced it. Something slid across the floor as she pushed the door partially open. Looking behind the door to see what had blocked it, she found several boxes had been stacked against it. Now, wariness turned to fear.

She whirled and started downstairs, but reason returned before she had gone far. This was her home, and she wasn't going to abandon any part of it to an unknown person. With a deep sigh to cover her fright, she turned back up the stairway. She stepped into the attic hallway, swallowed her panic. The light from one small window revealed a hall and two doors, one directly across from the other.

Her heart pounded in her ears and she licked lips that had suddenly gone dry.

"Which door, Tiger?" she whispered.

As if he understood, the cat padded with great certainty to the door on the right. Alexa followed, but her hands trembled and she fumbled at the doorknob. Tiger gave a little meow, as though asking her what was taking so long.

She swung the door open and raised the gun into shooting position. It didn't give her much confidence, though, when she looked down the shaking barrel.

The room in front of her was shadowy, but Alexa could see it was a tidy storage room. Everything was neatly boxed, wrapped, stacked, and labeled. A large floor-to-ceiling wardrobe occupied one full wall. If

13

someone were here, he must be hiding in that wardrobe. Alexa gulped and backed toward the door.

"Meow," Tiger commanded as he stood in front of the wardrobe, looking at her.

"Oh, dear Lord, please, please, help me," she pleaded softly.

Resting the gun on her hip, she edged toward the cupboard. Tiger gave an impatient scratch on its door. Pricks of fear ran from Alexa's head to her toes. Did she really want to know who was behind that door? She had no choice. She must assure herself that this was not someone who might murder her in her sleep or . . . worse.

Alexa grabbed the handle and pulled the door open. Nothing! The cupboard hung full of winter clothing, and the bottom was stacked with boxes. Using the gun barrel, she poked through the clothes, testing the space to the back of the closet. Each time she heard a solid thump against the back wall, she became more confident that this whole episode was a figment of her imagination. And then the barrel rammed into something soft and fleshy-feeling.

Alexa raised the gun to her shoulder. "Co—co—come out of there." It sounded more like a plea than a command.

The clothing stirred, and two hands and the top of a head appeared.

"Please, don't shoot," the frightened woman begged. Straightening before Alexa, her hands in the air, she continued in a trembling voice. "I didn't mean no harm. The house was empty, and I needed a place. Ain't done nothin' but good." She talked rapidly as though hoping if she explained fast enough, Alexa could be persuaded not to kill her on the spot.

The woman looked to be in her middle thirties, maybe older. Her coarse dress and shoes, unstyled hair, and work-calloused hands were mute testimony that her life hadn't been easy.

14

Lowering the gun, Alexa said, "Put your hands down. I won't shoot you. What's your name?" Her voice sounded firm, helping her to feel in control of the unusual situation.

"Emmie. Emmie Dugan." She winced, speaking barely above a whisper.

"Is that supposed to mean something to me?"

"My husband's the outlaw, Luke Dugan."

"If you have a husband, then what are you doing hiding out in an empty house?"

"The law's got 'im. Holdin' 'im in Coeur d'Alene. Aimin' to put him behind bars permanent, down in the penitentiary at Boise City. Maybe even hang 'im. I ain't got no money and no place to go. Don't know what I'm gonna do." She hung her head and stood, shoulders slumped, a picture of despair.

An idea crossed Alexa's mind. "What are you fit to do?" She moved toward the door after shutting the cupboard.

Emmie followed, keeping a safe distance from the gun. "I kin wash clothes, clean, cook. Things like that's about all. Don't nobody rich want someone that looks like me for the likes of that, though."

Alexa had to agree the missing front tooth and uncorseted figure didn't present a particularly appealing image. But Aunt Cassy would never have turned away such a pitiful person.

Accepting the challenge, Alexa said, "Well, I must have help doing the very things you mentioned. I was wondering how I was going to manage all this house and run a ranch, too. If you'll stay, I'll pay you twenty dollars a month and your room and board."

Emmie's face lit up like the sun breaking through storm clouds. "Ma'am, you won't be sorry. I'll work real good for you. And I'll stay as long as you like. My Luke's done got hisself in a peck o' trouble this time. Worst part is, he's innocent. Done plenty of wrong in his time, but he didn't do none of this."

15

"None of what?" Alexa asked as she led the way down the spiral staircase.

"None of the train robbin' and killin' the guard, and him bein' charged with the whole thing. Luke's a lot of things, but he's no killer. He wasn't near that train. We moved from Colorado and found a little cabin in the Selkirk Mountains up near the Canadian border. He was huntin' us some fresh meat, and he don't have no alibi. Witnesses say it was him held up the train, but they got him mixed up with someone else. We come here for a fresh start. Funny how things work out." She sighed. "Can't afford a lawyer, so he plans on hangin'."

Her voice sounded so tired and defeated it hurt Alexa. "It should give him some comfort to know you're being taken care of, at least."

"That's the last thing he said to me. 'Emmie, what's to become of you?' he said. He's a good man in a lot of ways. He's served the time to pay for his past sins and he was workin' hard at stayin' out of trouble. We ain't been married so long, but he settled in just fine. Wanted a permanent job with stock. He's real good with animals."

Emmie trailed Alexa downstairs. In the kitchen. Alexa stood the gun in the corner and asked, "Emmie, do you believe in the Lord?"

Emmie looked shocked by the question. "Yes'm," she said slowly. "My ma, God rest her soul, always read to us out of the Bible every Sunday. But I ain't talked with Him in years. Lord don't know the likes of me exists anymore."

"Oh, yes He does. We'll get down on our kness and do some talking to Him, and a way will come to help your Luke. I know it will."

"I wish I could believe that, ma'am. I truly do."

"You can truly believe that. Come, kneel here with me and I'll pray with you. He's the only one to trust with a problem like yours. He'll know exactly what to do about it."

16

Alexa grasped the work-worn hand, gently pulled Emmie to her knees, and prayed, "Dear Lord, we give thanks for Your great compassion as You seek the lost lambs. Today we come to You with a special request to help Luke Dugan. We know that if it is Your will, the truth will be made known about him and he will be set free. Comfort Emmie's heart and let her feel that, with faith, all things are possible."

As they said their final amens, the voices of men shouting greetings carried in through the open front door. Emmie leaped from her knees and raced across the hall to hide in a room Alexa had yet to explore.

Alexa advanced to the front porch where she could see a cloud of dust rising along the road. Over the rattling of an approaching buggy, she heard the hoofbeats of more than one horse as they came pounding toward her at a hard gallop.

Who would come calling at such an early hour? Nobody even knows I've arrived.

CHAPTER 2

ALEXA STOOD IN THE OPEN DOORWAY and watched as a buggy with a man and a woman clattered up the rutted road, accompanied by a horseman riding alongside on a shining silver-gray horse. The man in the buggy, whom she guessed to be in his late twenties, swung the shiny black vehicle about. Turning the high-spirited horse too late for safety, he nearly annihilated the red hollyhocks blooming profusely at the foot of the wide covered porch that encircled the house. His speed was such that he narrowly missed the wagon in which she had arrived. Alexa grew highly anxious for the well-being of the occupants before the buggy slid to a stop next to the porch steps, leaving clouds of choking dust in its wake. What manner of speed demon controlled the reins, she wondered? He must be slightly mad to drive so wildly with the delicate appearing older woman as a passenger.

Land, did people in the West always come calling so early? Anxious that she present a reasonably proper appearance, she nervously fingered the nape of her neck in search of escaped tendrils from the curls

18

in the upswept hairdo. She didn't wish to appear disheveled before her visitors, even at such an hour. First impressions lasted, Aunt Cassy always said.

Alexa did not respond well to the unexpected, perhaps because there had been so little in her life that hadn't been thought through and carefully planned. As a result, Alexa found it difficult to keep her composure at this moment.

The rough-looking man on horseback pulled up at a distance behind the buggy and appeared in no hurry to state his business. The woman, clearly a breath-taking beauty in her youth, and still quite stunning, shared the single seat with the tall, faultlessly groomed driver of the buggy. Alexa felt for a moment transported from this wild land back to the civilization of Illinois.

"How do you do, my dear," the smiling, silver-haired woman called. "I do hope you'll forgive our manners. This isn't a formal call."

Alexa breathed a sigh of relief at the bit of news and relaxed perceptibly.

"David and I were on our way to town and noticed an unfamiliar wagon here. We thought it best to stop in case strangers were making themselves at home."

She spoke with a New England accent and her bearing affirmed breeding and polish. Alexa wondered how the woman happened to be so far from her roots. "Thank you for keeping watch. I'm Alexa Spence."

"I thought you might be. We've waited anxiously for your arrival. I'm Jane Hornbeck and this is my son, David. We own the ranch bordering yours on the west."

Such lovely, gracious neighbors. Alexa welcomed this kind of surprise. She walked to the edge of the porch and extended her hand in greeting. From that vantage point she also noticed David Hornbeck's clear tanned skin and an impeccably trimmed blonde mustache.

Alexa spoke in the formal language of first acquaintance. "How do you do," she said to Mrs. Hornbeck. "It is a great pleasure to be here. I, too, have anticipated this day for several months."

Alexa couldn't recall ever having received such unabashed approval, and she felt herself blush.

"Have you ever been on a western ranch?" Mrs. Hornbeck asked.

Managing a bare minimum of control, she struggled for a coherent answer. "Not on a ranch. I was raised on a farm."

"I daresay you'll find ranching quite different. Are you planning to run it yourself?"

Alexa could almost hear the sniff of disdain beneath the words. Apparently Mrs. Honrbeck regarded ranching considerably above farming.

"Yes. Aunt Cassy says I'm a natural manager and this ranch should finally give me a challenge," Alexa replied. "But I'm sure I shall need guidance while I learn."

David's full lips parted in a smile that revealed nearly perfect white teeth, and his eyes creased deeply at the corners. She had trouble breathing as her rapidly beating heart seemed to take up far more than its alloted space.

Doffing a soft tan Stetson, and uncovering thick carefully barbered blond hair, he said, "A great pleasure to meet you, Miss Alexa." His voice, a fine, smooth baritone stroked each syllable of her name. "I would be more than happy to offer you my assistance any time you wish to begin."

At that moment the large saddle horse standing next to the wagon shook its head impatiently, and the jangle of the bit rings broke the spell. Alexa forced her attention to her other guest. He sat astride the striking gray stallion fitted with expensive tack. Alexa didn't knows a great deal about fine riding horses or their equipment, but she knew quality when she saw it. Even though the rider slouched in his saddle, she

20

could tell the man was tall. A wide-brimmed black Stetson sat well down on his mop of dark curly hair that had not seen a barber in far too long. Dark eyes above a full, black beard pierced hers, and his look held no welcome.

Mrs. Hornbeck turned and gave the man a decidedly cool smile. "Alexa, this is your neighbor to the east, Martin Taylor. He operates a logging operation that is rapidly scalping the land of its beautiful trees."

Holding out her hand to him, Alexa said, "How do you do?"

His only reply was a curt nod.

Anger flashed through her. *How rude*, she thought. Alexa quickly retracted her hand and clasped it together with the other one in front of her. She felt an immediate and intense dislike for the unmannerly clod.

Mrs. Hornbeck let her enjoyment of the little scene show in her twinkling eyes. "Well, my dear, we shan't detain you. You must have many things to do. When you've had a bit of time, we'll make a proper call. In the meantime, though, please don't hesitate to let us help you if we can." She smiled and gave a little wave of her leather-gloved hand. The gloves, Alexa noted, were the same shade as the beaver fur trimming on her cloak. Tying a piece of ecru netting over the toreador-styled hat, Mrs. Hornbeck looked fondly at her son. "Shall we go, David?"

David nodded in acknowledgment, but continued to let his gaze rest openly on Alexa's face, making no attempt to mask his pleasure at meeting her. "We're glad you've arrived safely," he said in a normal voice. "I shall call back this evening, to be certain everything is in order and make myself available in the event you need any help. I would be very glad to share my ranching experience with you."

"Thank you, Mr. Hornbeck. I shall look forward to that."

He smiled and nodded, then returned his hat to his head with a flourish. "Be sure to save the wood-cutting until I come." Gathering the reins, he expertly swung the buggy around, and clattered out of sight down the dusty road.

Alexa, much to her annoyance, was left alone with the unmannerly horseman. Even his dress irritated her. He wore a bulky red and black plaid shirt that could not hide his broad muscular shoulders. Dark gray pants tucked into work-scarred knee-high boots completed clothing that spoke his occupation. Leather-gloved hands holding the loose reins rested lightly on the saddle horn. The gun in a holster strapped around his waist disturbed her. She wished he would state his business and leave, for he obviously hadn't come to greet her. But he would have to talk outside. She had no intention of inviting him in.

"Miss Spence," he began very formally, "as Mrs. Hornbeck pointed out, I own the land to the east of your ranch. Your uncle and I agreed that we would mutually maintain the fence separating our property. I have been handling it all myself this spring."

Alexa opened her mouth to defend herself, but Mr. Taylor left her no opportunity.

"I have been willing to do this under the circumstances, even though it has taken men from my logging crew, slowing down my operation. However, there was another part to the agreement. Your uncle agreed that while his cattle were on the open range he would prevent them from grazing in the section of the forest where we were cutting. When cattle get in the way, it is hazardous to both animals and man. The woods where we're cutting are full of your stock this morning. I am *not* going to tend your cows any longer. I would appreciate it if you would take care of the problem."

Alexa drew herself up to her full five feet. "Sir," she began in a cold regal voice. "I have only just arrived. I do not see how you can expect me to be knowledgeable regarding the situation you describe, nor expect me to solve it immediately."

"That is why I explained the problem in some detail, so that you *would* be knowledgeable. Now, with your permission, I'd like to try to find that lazy bum who's supposed to watch the herd and get him out to round them up. There's plenty of good grazing all over the forest, but the beasts seem to like human company. Unless they're checked on frequently, they'll gravitate to where we're cutting every time. I don't relish cleaning up a flattened cow if one of those big cedars falls on it."

Alexa shuddered at the mental picture he drew. The man was a course individual, and he offended her sensibilities.

Standing in the high-noon sun, she was growing uncomfortably warm in her fully lined, woolen traveling suit. If this conversation didn't soon end, much as she resisted the idea, she would be forced to invite him inside for her own comfort.

"Am I to conclude that this negligent person is somewhere on my property?"

"He's probably passed out cold in the bunkhouse. If that's the case, I suggest you fire him and get a responsible cowboy. There are plenty around looking for work. In fact, I turned one away just this morning. Wanted to hire on as a logger. And what I don't need is a cowboy who thinks all you do is rope a tree and saw it down."

Even shaded as they were by the brim of his hat, she could see the glint of humor in his eyes. "Does it amuse you to find a lady in such a predicament?" she asked, keeping her voice cold and distant.

His expression immediately grew inscrutable and his voice a bit warmer. "No ma'am, it doesn't. But I believe in solving problems. It creates real hard feelings and misunderstandings when they're allowed to drag on." He shifted his weight and swung easily out of the saddle. "Mind if I tie the pony to your porch since there isn't a hitching post? I'll go with you to the bunkhouse. See if that miserable excuse for a cowboy is sleeping one off."

She looked down at her outfit. She wasn't going out through the weeds and brush in this suit. "The cattle have been in your way all morning. A few more minutes won't matter. If you'll be so kind as to help me carry in my luggage, I'll change, and we can go searching for my reluctant employee together."

Alexa wanted to laugh. The look on Mr. Taylor's face indicated he'd much prefer to find the errant cowboy, deliver his lecture, and be on his way. But there was no way she and Emmie could carry those heavy trunks and traveling bags. He was an opportunity sent from heaven, and she had no intention of letting him slip away.

He walked over and looked in the wagon. "You need all these?"

"Mr. Taylor, I would not have brought them all the way from Illinois if I had not. And as you can see, I can't possibly lift the trunks, much less carry them. If you would like, I'll take one end, for I know they're quite heavy."

His answer was to reach in and grasp a thick leather handle, testing the weight of the largest trunk. It was a square box made of basswood and covered with extra heavy duck cloth. Three evenly spaced hardwood slats ran the length and width of the trunk to give added strength. Its corners were bound with heavy brown leather and two thick leather straps banded the trunk and buckled in front. He turned to her, a heavy scowl darkening his face. "Tell me one man put this in here," he said in a way that let her know he'd recognize the lie if she answered yes.

"No. It took two people, huffing and puffing rather pathetically, as I recall." Then she added wickedly.

24

"Of course, one looked to be about seventy and the other was a boy."

He shot her a deadly glance, tipped his head, and hoisted the trunk over the side of the wagon and down to the ground. He did it so quickly and with such apparent ease she would never have known the effort put forth if the muscles and veins in his neck hadn't stood out dramatically under the strain.

"Where do you want this—second floor or the attic?" he asked, making no attempt to keep the sarcasm from his voice.

If he carried it up the steps and into the entrance hall without acquiring a rupture, he'd be lucky, but she intended to make his life as miserable as he was making hers. At least, for a few more minutes. "Attic," she answered curtly.

He re-set his hat, rubbed his gloved hands together, and grasped the leather handles on each side of the trunk. Even through his pants she could see the muscles in his legs distend as he lifted the load.

Suddenly, feeling guilty, she offered, "Here, let me take one end," and started down the steps toward him.

"Get out of the way," he growled.

It became abundantly clear she had pushed him almost too far. She ran into the house and without having any idea what was behind it, threw open the door across from the parlor entrance. "Thank you, Lord," she breathed as she stepped into a large bedroom. From the pipe still resting on the bedside table and the faint scent of bay rum that lingered, Alexa concluded this bedroom had belonged to Uncle Clyde.

She stepped back into the doorway as he entered the hall. "In here," she instructed briefly, her voice cool and distant. She had no intention of letting him know how badly she felt at having asked him to carry that terribly heavy piece of luggage. "Set it over by the window out of the way. I'll unpack it later."

She watched muscles ripple over his back as he carefully placed the trunk where she had indicated. Then without a word, he turned and retraced his steps to the buckboard for her other things.

When he reappeared with the suitcase containing her everyday dresses, she quickly opened it and selected a royal blue calico and a gingham-checked apron to match and laid them across the bed. Looking about for somewhere private to change, she noticed a door at the far end of the long room. Hurrying, she opened it and found herself staring into the most elegant bathroom she had ever seen. A six-foot copper-lined bathtub and an enamel wash basin set in a marble-topped oak cabinet drained to the outdoors. A commode of polished solid oak fitted with a galvanized bucket completed the elegant fixtures. Uncle Clyde had spared no expense in building or furnishing his home, she was rapidly discovering.

As she crossed the room for her things, Mr. Taylor, face red and shiny with sweat, came through the door with arms and hands loaded. "This looks like it, unless you have a freight wagon coming with the rest." His voice sounded much less angry. Perhaps he'd worked out his irritation at her.

Alexa gathered her dress and apron into her arms. "Excuse me, and I'll get into some work clothes. When I've changed, you can show me where the bunkhouse is, and we can see about my wayward help."

He nodded. "Mind if I get a drink?"

"I haven't had time to carry in fresh water. Do you know where the well is?"

"It's under the house. You have water indoors and a pump in the kitchen. In fact, there isn't a modern convenience Jane Hornbeck overlooked when she supervised the building of this house. Thought it was going to be hers." He disappeared through the door and she could hear his booted feet thudding down the

26

hall to the kitchen. Alexa dressed quickly and went to find her neighbor. He sat in the shade of the front porch, slouched in a rattan chair, casually picking his teeth with a straw. *Honestly,* she thought, *he has the manners of a goat.* Trained, however, to show the utmost courtesy to company, she put on a polite smile and said, "Are you ready?"

"Just waiting on you, ma'am," he answered casually, and languidly unfolded himself from the chair.

For a man who had been in such an all-fired hurry earlier, he surely took his time now, she thought as she watched him. He moved with a slow cat-like grace that fascinated her and only by exerting the greatest effort could she unfasten her gaze from him.

He led the way around the house and down a well-used trail that skirted a large clump of trees. He walked easily but steadily and his long legs covered a great deal of ground. Alexa found herself trotting behind him to keep up. She arrived breathless at the hired helps' gray weathered quarters that stood a discreet distance from the house.

Mr. Taylor didn't bother to knock. He flipped back the latch and threw open the door. His huge frame filled the doorway so she couldn't see a thing.

'What's there?" she asked.

"Just what I expected." He didn't move, as though deciding what action to take.

Alexa stepped closer to the doorway and a sour smell filled her nostrils. Before she could request he move so that she might see, he stepped back out and pulled the door shut.

"Why did you do that? Is there someone in there?"

"He's in there, all right, but it's no use trying to wake him now. The place is a mess and needs a thorough cleaning."

"Let me see."

"No." He set his body across the door. "I'll come back later and see that he cleans it up before he leaves. I really hate to fire the old boy. He's been on the ranch for years, but he's taken to drinking something fierce ever since Clyde died. Can't depend on him for a thing. Almost as bad— he's drinking up all his savings. Don't know what'll become of him.'' Compassion filled his voice, and Alexa realized that Mr. Taylor really liked the old man.

"I appreciate all your help, Mr. Taylor, but you don't have to fire him. He's my problem. I inherited him along with the rest of the ranch. Has he always had trouble with drink?''

"Not really, Miss Spence. He ties one on a couple of times a year, usually after the round-up and on New Year's. Never let it interfere with his job before, though. He's worked for Clyde since he started the ranch and can't seem to get over his death.''

They started walking back to the house, but this time Alexa led the way.

"Won't you come inside?'' she invited. "We still haven't settled the issue of my cattle in your forest.''

He untied the reins and gathered them preparatory to mounting. "I'll have my men run 'em back into the hills. In the meantime, I'll keep an eye out for someone to help you.'' He swung easily into the saddle and adjusted the reins. Then he sat, not signaling the horse to move.

Alexa wondered what she should do now. Had she missed a cue? Was he waiting for her to say goodbye, thank him again for unloading her luggage? Remembering the rebuff earlier, she reluctantly extended her hand again, and walked up to the mounted rider. "Thank you so much for your help, Mr. Taylor. I also appreciate your patience in dealing with my wandering stock. I hope I am soon able to resolve the problem of the cattle so you can get on with your work without fear of wiping out my herd.''

He looked down at her, his granite gray eyes glowed with a soft patina as they scanned her

28

upturned face. "Mind calling me Martin?" he asked, his voice deep and rich with overtones.

She felt the vibrations of his voice penetrate and pulsate through her. Felt his look pin her to the spot. Felt impaled by the emotions that surged through her. In the turmoil, she forgot he had asked a question.

He removed his glove and, leaning over the saddle, took her hand. His palm was warm and surprisingly uncalloused, but his strength flowed over her, leaving her renewed through its force. She ran the tip of her tongue over her dry lips, then dared to raise her eyes to his.

"You should never wear any color but blue. Turns your eyes to sapphires." His voice became a low throb that scattered her thoughts like rose petals in the wind. She stood dumb, her hand still resting in his, caught in the trance he induced so expertly. "I'll be back this evening to look in on our friend in the bunkhouse and chop you some wood."

She swallowed and hoped her voice wouldn't reveal the disquiet inside. "That's very kind of you, but I can attend to the poor man when he awakens, and Mr. Hornbeck has offered to stop by. I've put you to enough trouble for one day."

Martin's grip loosened, and he dropped her hand most unceremoniously. She watched his face grow hard and opaque, the eyes turn to slate. He pulled his hat hard over his eyes, set his mouth in a tight line, and wheeled his horse about. Without further words, he bent low and raced down the road at a full gallop.

Alexa stood dumb founded. What on earth had she said to bring about such a complete change in him? She would think more about it later, but right now she had a house to put to rights and a hired man to sober up.

CHAPTER 3

MUCH TO ALEXA'S DELIGHT, she found Emmie to be a hard worker. The woman learned quickly how Alexa wanted things done and strove mightily to do them that way. The clotheslines soon hung full of airing linens, and most of the windows in the house were thrown open to drive out the musty smell. By late afternoon the inside of the house had taken on a shine produced by vigorous scrubbing, dusting, and polishing.

Finished, they collapsed into chairs in the sitting room. "We have earned our keep this day," Alexa said, rolling down the sleeves of her dress and buttoning them at the cuffs. "Let's rest a minute and then while you start supper, I'll go up to the bunkhouse and see about that poor man. If he's well enough, I shall bring him down to eat."

Alexa laid her head against the high back of the rocking chair and relaxed. Her eyelids grew heavy, and she drifted off into unbidden sleep. Five chimes of the rosewood grandfather clock across the room wakened her. Stretching thoroughly, she drove sleep from her body so that she might be up and about her tasks. She could hear Emmie already busy in the kitchen.

Alexa stuck her head through the kitchen door. "You'd have let me sleep the night, wouldn't you?"

Self-conscious over the missing front tooth, Emmie flashed Alexa only a quick, flawed grin. "No, I'da made you eat, then sleep again. You're plumb tuckered, what with travelin' night and day and then doin' work in one afternoon that woulda took other folks days."

"I feel wonderfully refreshed by the little nap. Now I must go and see to our man. I shall be back in a few minutes. Be sure to set three places."

Alexa made her way across the freshly scrubbed pine plank floor, brightened with small multi-colored rag rugs and out onto the porch. A slight breeze brushed her cheek and brought the fragrance of wild roses growing in big scraggly bouquets about the yard.

Alexa walked slowly along the path, enjoying the view across a lovely meadow she had missed earlier as she trotted after Mr. Taylor. Several fine horses grazed there on grass already grown two feet high. Such an abundant stand would make good hay if she was able to find someone to cut and stack it. And if she could get two crops, she would have no worry about feed this winter.

Alexa raised her eyes to the sharp-edged mountain ridges twisting and turning in the distance. They might have been formed by gargantuan loggers, running among swinging huge axes, chopping ridge from ridge, and then with their hatchets, carefully trimming the high parts of the ridges into separate peaks. However, the appearance of all but the tallest mountains was softened by a mantle of deep perpetual green – the thousand-year old evergreen of trees—white pine and red cedar. The trees Martin Taylor was stripping from the land.

She arrived at the bunkhouse that stood shaded by tall firs, their rough bark moss-covered on the north. Standing with her hand on the latch, Alexa felt reluctant to face what she had only smelled previously. At last, determination won, and she knocked on the slab door. There was no answer and not a sound from inside to indicate anyone was there. She knocked again. Nothing. Lifting the latch, she pushed the door open a few inches, enough to stick her head through. The odor was gone, replaced by the unmistakable smell of strong lye soap. The place had been scrubbed, the bed made, and despite the somewhat crude, homemade appearance of a small unpainted table, four upright chairs, and a rocker, the room had a comfortable, lived-in air. But it was empty.

Pushing the door open all the way, she stepped up into the room. Behind the door she found his clothes hanging on pegs along the wall. Beneath these on the floor, stood a collection of cowboy boots in various stages of wear, from nearly new to ancient. *Well, if he's gone, he's traveling extremely light,* she concluded.

She felt the cookstove in the corner. It was cold, and there was no wood in the woodbox. She could find very little food in the cupboard, certainly not enough to prepare any kind of a meal. What had the old man subsisted on? Obviously, from the collection of bottles in the trash, his diet for some time had been mainly liquid. He must be a physical wreck and feeling wretched. Poor man!

Leaving, but making sure the door was securely latched behind her, she stood, hands on her hips, wondering where he might be. She would feel much more comfortable if she could locate and speak with him. In his present condition, he probably wouldn't prepare a suitable meal even if he had supplies. She wanted to be sure he had a proper supper.

It suddenly occured to her that she hadn't seen any

barns or other out-buildings. A ranch had to have a barn. Looking about, she located a well-used path leading through the trees. *Probably goes to the outhouse.* But since it was the only trail she could see, she started up the path anyway. A short distance into the woods, it forked. Having a tendency toward left-handedness, she chose the left fork and continued. The trail broke through the trees abruptly, and she was again in the meadow.

Now, however, instead of grazing horses, she faced two large red barns and several smaller buildings, also painted red and white. Beyond were numerous corrals and chutes.

Suddenly she realized the extent of the wealth Uncle Clyde had left her— not just the fine house and cattle—but this wide open space—to breathe, to be! She took a deep breath and threw out her arms in a spontaneous gesture.

Aunt Cassy had given her a rich heritage too— albeit one of learning to share too little with too many Now, here in Idaho, she could build on that foundation – could grow, mature, and with God's guidance, begin to repay her great debt by helping others as she had been helped.

As she stood absorbed in her thoughts, a bent old man tottered out of one of the buildings and, carrying a small bucket, hobbled into the barn nearest her. Galvanized to action, she hurried down the path and through the door he had entered.

It took a few minutes for her eyes to grow accustomed to the hazy, subdued lighting of the interior, but when she could see, she found him scattering grain to clucking, red-feathered chickens gathering around his feet. He talked softly to them and then when he finished, he sat down on a stump and watched them feed.

Alexa felt like an intruder as she watched the intimate moments, but the longer she looked, the more her desire grew to help this poor old man suffering such deep grief and distress. She cleared her throat and gave a tiny cough. He looked up quickly and, upon seeing her, struggled to his feet.

She stepped forward. "I'm Alexa Spence, Mr. Grant's niece."

He nodded and bowed slightly. "I'm Jake."

His answer, so brief and curt, caught Alexa by surprise. She had anticipated an explanation of his earlier behavior—perhaps even an apology. Why had she thought he would oblige her with all the information she wanted? Obviously, she was going to have to dig it out of him.

"Are you Uncle Clyde's hired man?"

"Yep."

He was being less than cooperative. To cover her increasing discomfort she asked, "How are you feeling?"

"Fine."

Well, this wasn't getting her anywhere. Perhaps if she could get him into more favorable surroundings, she might learn something of him and the ranch. He was the only one who could really tell her about the daily routine. "I would like you to come to the house for supper," she insisted. "We need to talk about your plans, which I hope include continuing to work for me."

He looked extremely uncomfortable. "Don't eat at the big house. Eat in the bunkhouse," he mumbled.

"It would please me greatly if you'd consider making an exception tonight. I need to know the details of ranching and I am at a loss to know where to begin."

He stood shuffling his feet and clenching and unclenching his hands. Finally, as she was about to give up, he said, "Guess I can, this once, seeing as you're in need of help."

"Thank you. I appreciate your accepting the invitation. We'll eat in about a half an hour." Alexa turned and nearly ran out the door before he had second thoughts and changed his mind. She hurried back along the path to the house, her thoughts on how best to get Jake to talk to her. If he had been with Uncle Clyde all those years, this must seem like home to Jake. She wanted him to continue to feel that way. Move on when it was his choice, not from having to. But how could she get him to stop drinking? She would not put up with that. There were too many things needing attention. In fact, it seemed to her, she needed more help. She and Emmie could take care of the house and garden, but the ranch itself was too large for one man to run properly. And an old, drunken one at that.

Arriving in the clearing where the house stood, she paused. Tied to the front porch stood a fine pony fitted with a well-used saddle and a bedroll strapped across the back. Sitting on the front steps was a middle-aged man dressed much as she had seen Jake, the boots with specially designed heels to keep the feet from slipping through the stirrups, denims, and a slip-over cotton shirt. A famous western-cut Stetson hat was pulled far over his eyes. It took a couple months' wages to buy a Stetson, but she knew no self-respecting cowboy, no matter how poor, would be seen in public without one.

The stranger sat rolling a stick between his fingers and apparently looking at the step between his feet. When he became aware of Alexa, he leaped up and removed his hat. "Afternoon ma'am. You Miss Spence?"

Perhaps this was the cowhand Mr. Taylor had promised to send over. He had left in such a state, she wasn't sure that he would remember his promise.

"I am," she said and moved quickly to the steps. Alexa liked the no-nonsense look about this man. He stood less than six feet, but his erect bearing made him appear taller. He didn't seem to limp or favor any part of his anatomy as she had seen so many cowboys do as they got off and on the train during her trip west. She scanned the stocky, well-muscled body. He would be able to throw a cow to brand and do the heavy work. Hopefully, he didn't drink to excess.

"Martin Taylor sent me over. Said you could use an extra hand."

Thank you, Lord, for knowing what I needed before I did and for providing.

So, Mr. Taylor had sent him. Did that mean he had forgiven her for whatever it was she had done to make him angry? She hoped so. She didn't want trouble with a neighbor. "Yes, I need a permanent extra hand, one that won't pick up and leave just before round-up. One who can handle a crew."

"I can do that, ma'am. And I'd like to try out that permanent arrangement. I ain't been permanent nowhere for so long, I can't remember when the last time was. Name's Bill Smith."

"Pleased to have you here, Bill. The bunkhouse is over through the trees. You'll be sharing the space with Jake. He's a fixture around here. Going through a bad time since my uncle died."

"Taylor told me a little about the place and the situation, you being new and all. I'll make peace with Jake. You'll have no worry."

"Good. Supper'll be ready in a few minutes."

He looked stunned. "Ma'am, not meaning no offense, but I'm not used to eating in the big house. If there's a stove at the bunkhouse, I can stew up some satisfactory vittles."

"There's a stove, but I don't think there's anything to stew up. When I return the wagon to the livery stable in town tomorrow, I'll do some grocery buying. Emmie found enough canned things to make supper tonight, and Jake's coming down."

Bill looked puzzled. "Emmie?"

36

"Her husband's . . . well, she needs a place to stay right now. She's going to be my housekeeper."

"Real nice of you to do that for her, ma'am. Real nice."

Why does this stranger care about Emmie? Oh, it's probably not Emmie. He figures I've a soft heart good for a loan or something. "She's doing as much for me. I need her help with this big house to run and the ranch to oversee."

He peered over his shoulder and strained to see down the porch. Alexa wondered at his action, but before she could inquire, he gave a shrug and mounted his horse. "See you at supper," he said. As he trotted off in the direction of the bunkhouse, Alexa noticed that he continued looking back over his shoulder. *What is he looking for?*

Alexa insisted that dinner be served in the dining room despite Emmie's timid objections. She had thought Emmie didn't want the bother, but after a quiet awkward meal during which the men spoke briefly only when spoken to, and then left hurriedly after, she realized Emmie knew far more about these people than she.

She helped Emmie with the dishes and then went to sit on the porch. Emmie disappeared immediately afterwards on her own errands, and Alexa was truly alone for the first time that day—alone to think and plan. She decided it would be wise to pay more attention to Emmie's instincts. She seemed to possess a primitive wisdom. Tonight, Alexa had learned absolutely nothing about either of the men or any details of running the ranch.

Since she hadn't been able to visit with Jake, she was going to have to devise another plan to reach him. Tomorrow, she would go to the bunkhouse and talk with them both, maybe even have supper there.

Tiger jumped into her lap purring contentedly, and

she rocked slowly in the man-sized cane and mahogany rocker and wondered if this was how Uncle Clyde spent his evenings after the day's work was finished. Looking down, she noticed a worn spot where her feet rested and knew he had.

Relaxing against the chair, she watched the red-orange sun drop slowly into its nighttime pocket in the mountains to the west. The air filled with bird calls, and in the distance she could hear her horses whinny. There was an answering neigh close by, and she looked to see David Hornbeck riding up on a shining chestnut.

"Hello!" he called.

She rose quickly and went to meet him at the front steps. "Hello, yourself. This is a nice surprise."

When he dismounted and came to stand next to her, she saw he wasn't as tall as Mr. Taylor, though he stood close to six feet.

"There shouldn't be any surprise. I told you I'd be back this evening." His dark brown eyes roamed at will over her face, and he made no attempt to hide the pleasure he received at what they saw. "I always keep my promises," he said, his voice warm and intimate.

Suddenly flustered, Alexa fumbled with the collar of her dress and smoothed the hair at the back of her neck. "But it was growing so late, I thought perhaps something had come up to detain you." She led the way to the spot on the porch where she had been sitting.

"Unfortunately, something did come up, but I have good men and they took care of it."

She indicated the chair next to hers. "What sort of problem did your men have at this hour?" she asked, genuinely interested in the answer. Soon, she must learn all she could about ranch affairs.

He moved the chair so he could see her clearly and sat. "The spring runoff is slowing and some of my

38

cattle were out of water. We had to move them onto the public range. They'll be grazing alongside yours now."

The tone of his voice was far from conversational and each syllable sent little pulses of excitement through her. Learning about ranching from him was going to be an experience to look forward to. One small thing bothered her, though. Withhighly polished boots, white shirt, and ever present tan Stetson he appeared to be a very prosperous cowboy yet his hands didn't look like he had ever done a day's work in his life. He was a puzzlement.

The sun was now safely stored for the night, and a soft pink-orange afterglow filled the western sky. Alexa and Mr. Hornbeck sat silent, listening to the birds begin their subdued evening chirping.

"Between the dark and the daylight, when the night is beginning to lower, Comes a pause in the day's occupations, That is known as the Children's Hour," he quoted softly.

Alexa turned to face him. "I, too, love Mr. Longfellow's poems and you have quoted one of my favorites."

"Mother used to entice me from my play with that verse. Then she would read to me, and we would play games before I prepared to retire. It's a rare evening that verse doesn't still run through my head."

He turned, smiled, and met her gaze. She was unaccustomed to such a frank display of esteem and it flustered her. She quickly raised her eyes to the deepening sunset. "Uncle Clyde has a wonderful collection of books. I've only just scanned the titles, but I'm anxious to begin reading them." Her voice came out in a breathless rush.

"I've shared many of those books with him," David Hornbeck nodded. "He and I exchanged reading material on a regular basis. I'd like to begin sharing them with you. However, I came to chop

39

some firewood for you tonight. I'd better get to it before it gets too dark." He stood up as he spoke and walked toward the wood pile a short distance from the house. Obviously, his offer had not been an idle one.

Having recovered her poise, Alexa rose and hurried to his side. "Oh, please don't bother! The woodbox was full when I arrived. And now that I have a new hired man, he can cut more tomorrow."

Thus reassured, David Hornbeck returned to the porch. "So you fired old Jake?"

He sounded almost glad at the idea. This also bothered Alexa. There were many undercurrents here that she could feel, but couldn't yet make sense of. She began to realize, however, that she was going to have to keep her wits about her until she learned what was going on.

Working to forget her annoyance, she answered in a soft voice, "Oh, my no. I couldn't do that. Poor man is heavy with grief. He's been behaving badly, I know, but he'll get straightened out. With Uncle Clyde gone, there's too much work for one man. The new man Mr. Taylor sent over will be a help to us both."

"Taylor sent him over, did he?" A cutting edge crept into his voice. "Taylor has no business interfering in the running of your ranch. He'd do well to tend to his own operation."

His voice, hard and sharp in contrast to the earlier warm vibrant tones, pierced her, leaving her cold. Was it possible these two men were jealous of each other? Each had reacted when the name of the other was mentioned. It seemed a highly likely supposition, she decided, given that each man was unmarried, ambitious, and in an occupation that, if expanded, could destroy the other.

Mr. Hornbeck stood suddenly. "I must be going. It will be dark soon and I have no light." He didn't even wait for her, but stalked along the porch, his steps echoing in the still evening air.

Dismayed that she might have offended him in some way, she hurried after him. "I'm sorry you have to leave so soon, but I fully understand. Thank you for coming all this way to chop my wood. I apologize for the inconvenience I've put you to," she said when she caught up with him.

He stopped on the second step and took her hand, rubbing the back of it with his thumb as he spoke. "Forgive me, Miss Alexa. I was rude just now. Your uncle talked of you so often that I felt I knew you well enough to share my deepest feelings. Martin Taylor is calloused and insensitive, intruding on everyone's lives in the valley. I find myself vexed whenever his name is mentioned."

Now he slowly turned her hand palm up, bowed, and pressed his lips into it. Her hand trembled as she felt the warm flesh of his lips and soft mustache brushing the cup of her hand. In Illinois, this would be frowned upon as fast and loose, but it seemed perfectly normal under the bright evening star rising in the pale blue afterglow of an Idaho sky.

She leaned against the porch railing to steady her weak knees. Then, gently he placed a parting kiss on the inside of her wrist. How glad she was she had taken a minute to dab a bit of persian lilac cologne there.

"Thank you for a special time. I will be over soon again," he promised. Mounting his horse in one flowing movement, he doffed his hat to her, and then galloped away.

She sat down on the steps and hugged her knees. She wanted to capture forever the lovely feelings running through her.

Later, as she undressed for bed, she could still feel the soft brush of his mustache and the imprint of his lips tingling in the palm of her hand. She lay sleepless with her hand open on her pillow. She felt the soft full moon steal the special tingle from her hand and seal it into her heart.

CHAPTER 4

LIFE ON THE RANCH QUICKLY settled into a routine. Jake, too crippled with arthritis to ride a horse with ease, tended the chickens, chopped wood, and became general handyman. He built the hitching post Alexa wanted, and a fence around the yard. She then instructed him in how to plant flowers and a garden.

Bill took over the range stock, haying, and the heavy work of the ranch. Martin Taylor had a good eye for men. Bill proved to be a hard worker, steady and dependable. He even gave Jake a powerful talking to about the evils of drink and refused to let him have a bottle. Alexa had happened to overhear this particular discussion and the intensity with which Bill spoke lingered with her. She hoped an opportunity would present itself to ask him about his experience with liquor.

Emmie and Alexa shared the housework, cooking, and gardening. Alexa set the table in the sitting room and insisted the men eat their meals at the big house. They worked long hard hours and she felt it was too much for them to prepare substantial meals. She could have hired a cook, but that seemed foolish for just two. When it came round-up time and there was a big crew, then she planned to have a full-time cook for the bunkhouse.

Alexa found herself with more and more work, and less and less leisure time. In fact, one morning a couple of weeks after her arrival, Alexa mutinied and stayed abed. She realized that she had trapped herself with all her plans. It occured to her that she had seen very little of her ranch. She had no idea what lay beyond the fenced meadow or how far her holdings spread. Today seemed a fine time to do some exploring.

There was just one small problem with her idea. She didn't know how to ride a horse, at least not very well. Aunt Cassy had declared such a pursuit unlady-like, and with Alexa alone among twelve boys, she was raised to be a lady. A very proper lady who didn't play tennis, ride horseback, square dance —anything "common" people did. Bless Aunt Cassy. She thought she was doing the right thing, but many times Alexa had chafed under the restrictions laid down by the dear woman.

Well, she couldn't blame her bondage on Aunt Cassy any longer. Hurriedly, she dressed in an old flowered calico dress. If she took a tumble or soiled it beyond washing clean, there would be little loss. Gulping down hot cereal kept warm in a double boiler on the back of the stove, Alexa bade Emmie goodbye and in her eagerness, flew to the barn.

As she entered the barnyard, she saw the chickens, and they reminded her of the blue ribbon Rhode Island reds she had raised back home. Even in her rush, she had to stop a minute and watch them scratching and clucking contentedly. As she stepped into the dusty, dimly lighted barn, she savored the smell of sweet hay, remnants of which still remained in the loft above. She must get a cow. She did miss the fresh milk, butter, and cream. Canned milk would do in a pinch, but as a steady replacement, it fell short.

She began a serious hunt for the tack room in search of a side-saddle. She found the room without much trouble, but look as she would, there seemed to be no woman's saddle. This was frustrating for it would delay her investigation of her holdings. Hopefully, there was a store in town that carried sidesaddles in addition to their regular line of stock saddles. She decided to catch a buggy horse, drive in, and find out. Grabbing a bucket of oats and a halter, she started out through the meadow toward the peacefully grazing horses. She hadn't quite reached the herd when she became aware of an approaching horse, its shod feet and jangling reins disrupting the quiet.

She looked about until she spied the horseman. "Mr. Hornbeck!" she gasped aloud. Her eyes dropped to her faded old dress. What would he think? But he had seen her and was already riding in her direction. There was no escape.

When he was close enough, he called, "Good morning, Miss Alexa. What are you up to, standing way out here holding a bucket of oats? Have I interrupted something?" He dismounted, dropped the reins so his horse could graze, and walked over to her.

"I was on my way to catch a buggy horse and drive to town. I very much want to learn to ride a horse and there seems to be no appropriate saddle in the barn. I thought perhaps I might be able to purchase one." He stood so near she could smell the clean, warm scent of him, fresh starched clothes mingled with the pungent odor of leather.

He flashed a wide smile. "You won't find a sidesaddle for sale in town. Don't stock them. It has to be ordered from a saddle maker and then he has to have to time to make it. Takes awhile for a new one, but we have several well-used models at the ranch. Let me help you bring in a good horse. Then, I'll go back to the ranch and pick up a saddle. It would give me a great deal of pleasure if you'd allow me to teach you to ride.''

"That seems a considerable amount of trouble,'' she objected politely, secretly delighted at his suggestion.

"No trouble at all. I came by to see if I could be of help in some way. Also, Mother wanted me to find out if you were ready for a formal call.''

Alexa thought a moment. "Would you ask her if next Tuesday is convenient?''

"I'll relay the question.''

Alexa kept her distance as David took the oat bucket and halter and expertly captured a fine-looking sorrell grazing nearby. Leading the horse back to her, he said, "I seem to remember this mare as being tame. Don't want to start you out on something eager to cut for the hills.''

They walked slowly together toward the barn. "I'll be back in about a half hour with the saddle. That'll give you time to get acquainted with the old girl.''

"And how do I make myself known to a horse?''

"By grooming her and talking to her while I'm gone. The two of you should be good friends by the time I return.' " He tied the horse in a stall, waved, and disappeared through the door.

Alexa stood outside the stall, eyeing the huge animal. "You certainly look a lot bigger inside than you did out in the pasture. I do wish Mr. Hornbeck hadn't tied you in here. I have no desire to walk past your heels to get to your head." Alexa found the curry comb and brush in the tack room, but how was she going to get next to the mare to brush her?

She decided to climb the wall of the adjoining stall and reach over into the mare's stall. When Mr. Hornbeck returned, Alexa, sitting on the divider between the stalls, had overcome her initial fright and was visiting happily with the docile animal as she brushed her.

Mr. Hornbeck set the saddle on a sack of grain. "I realized after I left that I should have tied her outside. You're a bit small to reach her back easily."

Alexa jumped down. "But as you see, Mr. Hornbeck, the problem is easily solved."

"Yes, Miss Spence, you are a clever woman." He untied the horse and brought the animal to stand next to the saddle.

He had called her Miss Alexa earlier, and she found this return to formality distressing. "Mr. Hornbeck, since we are neighbors and bound to see a great deal of one another, I would be pleased if you called me Alexa."

"Thank you, Alexa," he said, and then turned laughter-filled eyes on her. "I've longed to drop the formality myself."

The few dates Aunt Cassy found suitable for Alexa had been with gangling farm boys whose manners were bungling and whose speech seemed limited to words of one syllable. David's manners and maturity filled her with delight, and just gazing at him gave her pleasure.

She held the halter rope while David put the blanket and saddle in place. "I'm sure I could never lift that saddle," she said as she watched him swing the awkward-looking contraption to the back of her horse.

"I'm sure you couldn't. You'll need help when you want to ride. You have only to inform me of your plans, and I shall be right over." His dark eyes locked into hers and she felt an unwelcome blush rise. "You blush more beautifully than anybody I've ever seen," he said as he took the rope from her hand and replaced it with leather reins.

Alexa lowered her head and David responded with a chuckle, soft and rolling. She escaped the emotionally charged moment by leading the mare outside. There she met Jake as he came from around one of the

46

buildings. "Howdy," he greeted them. "See you gonna give old Molly a workout. She needs it. Just been growing fat and sassy out there in the pasture."

"With David's help, I'm going to try," Alexa said.

"Looks to me like you're a mite short in the limbs," Jake said as he appraised Alexa. "There's a stump over there you can use to board her."

"Come on, Molly, let's you and me get started on this lesson," Alexa urged as she pulled Molly toward the stump.

"What do you know about riding?" David asked.

"Precious little."

"I do hope you'll forgive me, but it is necessary to refer to certain parts of your anatomy. I shall attempt to be as delicate as possible." He waited for her to digest his warning and give her permission.

"I trust your judgment."

"Thank you." Clearing his throat, his face took on an impersonal look and his voice became crisp and business-like. "You mount and dismount on the left side. The upper crutch is a few inches to the left of the center line of the saddle and curved upward so as to hold your right limb in a secure and comfortable grip."

Alexa nodded her head, controlling the waves of shock at the mention of her limbs. While she knew nothing about a sidesaddle, she already doubted his casual remark that she would be secure and comfortable.

"The downward curving horn fitted to the saddle below the upper crutch is called the leaping-horn. It curls down and holds your left limb in place. In a crisis, you can stay in place by gripping downwards with your right limb against the upper crutch while drawing your right foot back, and pressing upward with your left limb against the leaping-head."

He said it all in such a nonchalant manner, Alexa knew he had never sat such a saddle. She wished for a

47

women to tell her how she could perch on that ridiculously small piece of leather, with her legs wrapped around two proturberances, and not fall off the moment the horse moved.

"Let me hold the reins and you get up on the stump. Put your left foot in the stirrup and rise into the saddle. Tuck your right extremity around the upper crutch." He pointed to the v-shaped object jutting out high on the front of the saddle.

She placed her foot in the stirrup as he directed, but when she tried to set her weight on the saddle, it moved. "Oh," she gasped, retreated immediately to the stability of the stump, and glanced wildly at David.

"If I cinch the saddle so tight it won't move, Molly will feel cut in half. Don't worry, it won't slip off."

Reassured, Alexa tried again. This time she succeeded in getting into the saddle seat and her leg hooked up over the crutch. *What an uncomfortable arrangement.*

"Bring your left extremity up against the leaping-horn," David instructed.

She did as he told her, then watched as he shortened the stirrup until her thigh was in contact with the underside of the leaping horn. She felt like a pretzel.

"The big problem with sitting a sidesaddle is both rider and saddle are fundamentally unbalanced. You must keep your weight positioned directly over the horse's spine, or the horse will develop a sore back. To compensate for everything being on the left side, you must consciously put most of your weight on the right. Imagine there is a tintack sticking up on the left side of the seat of the saddle, and you must avoid sitting on it."

Alexa pictured a large sharp point rising from the left of the saddle and immediately rose away from it.

"Splendid!" David cheered. "One more thing, and

you'll be ready. You must sit as squarely in the saddle as possible, with your body and shoulders facing perfectly forward.''

Alexa squared her shoulders and shifted her hips to the front. This made a terrible kink under her left rib cage as she stretched away from the tintack and faced forward.

"You look wonderful. You're going to be a natural at riding," David praised.

She smiled at his encouragement, but she watched with envy as David swung easily onto his stock saddle and settled himself astride his horse. Why was she nested on top of Molly like a fashionable hat? And she wasn't even anchored with hat pins. She looked with longing at his saddle horn. She had nothing to hold on to, and she desperately wanted to clutch something as David commenced leading the horse around the barn yard and corral.

She began to feel the gait of the steady mare and let her body rock with it. Round and round they went until Alexa felt not only comfortable, but bored.

"Are you ready to try your own reins?" David finally asked.

"I think so. I'm going to sleep, sitting up here and rocking along."

He handed her the reins but continued to hold the halter rope as a precaution. "You gently pull the rein on the side you want the horse to go," David instructed.

"No need to pull," Jake, working nearby, spoke up. "She's neck broke."

"So much the better," David answered. "Then you lay the rein across her neck on the opposite side. Here, give it a try."

David reached up and pulled the rein across the right side of Molly's neck. The horse turned her head to the left. Alexa understood, so she clucked Molly into a slow walk and practiced reining her. She and

49

the horse soon understood each other very well. But this saddle was a torture device developed, she was sure, by a man who wanted to get even with women.

"Do women ever ride in saddles like yours?" she asked David.

His head swiveled and his mouth dropped. "Women, I suppose, but no lady does."

"Well, this lady thinks this sidesaddle is terribly uncomfortable."

"You'll get used to it. Mother spends full days riding sidesaddle. My western saddle isn't rocking-chair comfortable, either, when you're first starting out."

So much for the idea she might ride astride. Yet, it wasn't only the comfort she craved. She simply didn't feel in control of the horse. If she had both knees around Molly and a saddle horn to grasp, Alexa knew she would have more control.

"Well, I think you've had enough for one day. You'll be stiff and sore tomorrow if we don't stop now." David guided Molly to Alexa's mounting stump and extended a hand to help her off.

Obediently, Alexa allowed him to unsaddle Molly and turn her back into the pasture. All the while he worked, she felt as she had with Aunt Cassy. Her life was being run by someone else. When was she ever going to have control, to do what she wanted, when she wanted, where she wanted? She hadn't planned to take her first riding lesson by walking around and around the barn yard. She had seen the barn and corrals, many times. She wanted to see her ranch.

"Are you going to be busy tomorrow?" she asked.

He hoisted the saddle onto his hip. "I'm sorry to say, I am. We have to move cattle. Probably take us the better part of the week." He must have noticed her face drop, because he added. "I'll have some free time next week if you'd like another lesson," he said before starting into the barn at a brisk pace. He

50

stopped and turned as though just remembering his message. "By the way, Mother would like to come calling next Tuesday, if that's agreeable with you."

She caught up with him at the tack room door and followed him inside where he put the saddle on a V-shaped rack protruding from the wall. "I'd be delighted!" But Alexa was thinking, *A whole week to sit and clean and weed*, and she narrowly prevented a deep sigh from escaping.

She didn't want David to leave. They were just beginning to feel comfortable together. "Won't you stay for dinner?" she asked, hoping that they could continue the lovely day.

He turned to face her and taking both her hands, drew her close to him. "I can't think of anything I'd rather do, but I have to go into town. Promised the bank I'd stop by and sign some papers. Then it's back to the ranch and herding cattle."

"It seems you spend a great deal of time with your cattle. Unless Bill isn't telling me something, all he does is keep mine away from Mr. Taylor's lumbering operation. Am I doing something wrong?"

"No. You don't have any problems. You have the best meadow land and water of anyone around. The rest of us in the valley are very envious of your situation." He tucked her hand into the curve of his arm, and they walked out into the sunshine.

"How many people live in our valley?" she asked as David gathered the reins of his horse and led him as they strolled slowly toward the house.

"A surprising number when you count the loggers and miners. The ranch folks and town people don't do much socializing with them, though. They're a rough unmannerly lot for the most part and prefer their liquor and women to our square dances and socials."

Alexa was having a hard time concentrating on what he was saying. All her senses were tuned to the feel of him next to her. He seemed to radiate security and protection. She knew she would never have to worry about anything with him around. The sound of his cultivated voice enfolded her like a cocoon, making the words he spoke seem of little importance. He brought her to a stop at the foot of the back door porch steps.

He turned her about so she stood opposite him. "I don't want to leave. I'd very much like to stay for dinner. I hope you understand that."

She looked into his sable brown eyes, soft and inviting, like magnets drawing her helplessly into their depths. She found herself inwardly straining toward him, knowing her eyes were begging him to kiss her and powerless to control their message. In her mind Alexa knew this was inappropriate behavior; her heart *refused* to let her behave properly. She had grown bored playing coquettish games with boys she cared nothing about. David was a man with everything she had ever dreamed of. They had so much in common, from bordering ranches to a love of poetry and literature. It seemed dishonest to deny her feelings.

She closed her eyes and allowed him to gently cup her face in the palm of his hand. He bent low over her, taking her waiting lips in a brief tender kiss. The emotion he stirred flowed through her like warm honey, leaving her unsatisfied, wanting more. Opening her eyes and searching his face, she saw a longing for her change the planes of his face.

Still holding her face, letting his thumb caress her cheek, he watched her intently. Clearing his throat before he spoke, he said, "There's a valley square dance a week from this Saturday at the schoolhouse. There'll be bidding on box lunches to raise money to remodel the teacherage. Would you do me the honor of attending?"

"Oh, David. That sounds wonderful! Our box socials in Illinois were such fun."

"They are here, too." His voice and the way he looked at her held future promises.

52

David seemed reluctant to let her go, but at last he released her and mounted the patient chestnut. "I'll see you before then. I'll try to bring mother when she comes to call on Tuesday. If I can't make it, I'll ride over some evening." He paused as if suddenly realizing she had issued no invitation. "That is, if it's all right with you."

She reached her hand up to him. "You know it is, David. Anytime."

He took the proffered hand and kissed the palm the way she remembered. The tremors again flocked through her, sending her heart into unrhythmic beats and leaving her breathless.

"Goodbye," he whispered softly as he folded her fingers over the kiss to protect it. "See you soon. Maybe sooner than you expect." With those words, he turned and rode away. This time, though, he kept looking back over his shoulder to where she stood with the hand holding his kiss closed tightly.

CHAPTER 5

THE REST OF THE DAY, whenever Alexa thought about David, she could feel his kiss on her mouth and in her hand. She would have floated totally out of control had not a hard little rock of uneasiness kept irritating her mind. She refused to let it surface, but it remained tenaciously disturbing.

After supper, when she and Emmie were finishing the dishes, Alexa took courage and mentioned an idea that had been forming all day. "Have you ever seen a lady ride a western saddle?" she asked, trying to keep her voice casual.

Emmie peered at her from under heavy dark brows. "Not what *you're* meaning by a lady."

Alexa was confused by Emmie's remark. What other kinds of ladies were there? One was either a lady or one wasn't. "Then you *have* seen ladies ride them. What kind of ladies?"

"Outlaw ladies," Emmie said curtly, and gave the dish towel a resounding snap before she hung it to dry.

"Oh," was all a subdued Alexa said, her hopes thoroughly dashed.

Emmie cast Alexa a disapproving look and stomped out of the kitchen on her nightly errands, whatever they were. Alexa walked slowly out onto the porch and sat down in her rocker. Tiger, waiting for his evening stroking, jumped into her lap and curled up. "Tiger, do you know I have never, never in my whole life done something I wanted to do if there was danger of censure. I have been the best, most obedient, dutiful person I know. And I'm sick of it!"

"Meow," Tiger responded.

"I quite agree. It's about time I started doing some of the things I want to do. Before I know it, I'll have lived my whole life and never been me. What I've been is a coward, afraid of risking someone's rebuke."

Tiger stood up, stretched, licked her hand, and laid back down.

"You're absolutely right. I've been licking hands long enough. I am not going to ride a horse on that miserable sidesaddle. If the whole valley wants to talk, they can. Give them something to chew on."

Gathering Tiger up in her arms, she marched through the house and up to the attic. She hadn't returned there since her first day when she had found Emmie hiding in the clothes cupboard. It was about time to explore its secrets.

She put Tiger down and he immediately started sniffing likely mouse retreats. Alexa opened the cupboard. A thorough examination revealed a collection of expensive men's clothes. These must have been placed here after Uncle Clyde died. Undoubtedly Mrs. Hornbeck had seen to it. However, there was nothing Alexa could wear or even make over.

The boxes placed under the eaves, labeled and stacked carefully, might produce some fabric or even some women's clothes. Alexa turned to these, but it was growing too dark to see. She could get a lamp, but if it accidentally tipped over or dropped, there was a good chance of burning down her house. Nothing was worth that risk. She couldn't do anything about a riding costume tonight, but that would be her first project in the morning.

When Alexa awoke, her back had a painful crick to remind her of yesterday's horseback ride. It also reinforced her decision to make a riding skirt and sit astride Molly.

Alexa found Emmie weeding the garden, a large poke bonnet hiding her face from the sun. When she heard Alexa, she raised up. "You know, Miss Alexa, if you'd quit tearing around in the hot sun without a bonnet, you wouldn't grow such a crop of freckles."

Her remarks and tone of voice stopped Alexa short. Emmie sounded just like Aunt Cassy. "I wore a bonnet everywhere I went for years. It didn't help that much. Besides you can't see but straight ahead when the poke sticks out so far."

"Turn your head, 'lessen your neck won't twist," Emmie said in a sour voice, and went back to her weeding.

Alexa bent to help Emmie, but her mind kept returning to her riding skirt. And she wasn't going to wear a bonnet, either. She pictured herself on Molly, riding across the meadow wearing a lace-trimmed flowered bonnet. She almost laughed aloud at the scene.

"You eaten anything?" Emmie asked.

"No, but I'm not hungry. I'll be fine until dinner. What do you want me to do now?"

Emmie picked up the hoe and leaned on it. "I hate to say this, and I don't mean no offense, but I'd be a lot happier if you'd find something else to use your time and stay outta my kitchen. I ain't used to help. Just keep tripping over your skirts." Emmie ducked her head and tightened her body as though waiting for blows to fall for having been so forward.

This was the longest speech Alexa had heard Emmie make and she hadn't known that Emmie had it in her. Likewise, she hadn't known she wasn't wanted as a helper. Alexa hugged her. "Thanks, Emmie. I really don't like housework or cooking. I was doing it because I thought I should. I can find a lot of things more to my liking."

Feeling like a child given a reprieve from chores, Alexa dashed off to the house and up the stairs to the attic. Throwing open the clothes cupboard, she found the boxes labeled hats and began opening them. They were filled with different colored Stetsons, some new or nearly so, and some well-worn.

She took out one of the new ones and tried it on. With a little padding inside the headband, it would fit. It had a number of colors and would go with any outfit she might choose to wear and keep the sun from growing so many freckles on her face. She didn't like admitting it, but Emmie was right. Alexa was beginning to produce a prize-winning crop as a result of her open rebellion against protecting her skin, either with parasol or bonnet. Aunt Cassy would have a fit if she could see her.

Setting these aside, she turned her attention to other boxes. Examining the labels, she finally located one marked fabric. With trembling hands, she unstacked boxes until she reached it. Excitement turned her fingers to thumbs, and she fumbled badly in her attempts to untie the twine. At last, she lifted the lid. There, folded in neat piles, lay an assortment of linen, cotton, velvet, and calico fabric. No worsted. She couldn't imagine riding with a calico or linen skirt. Velvet would look lovely, but not for long.

She left this box open and continued reading labels. No more fabric. Discouraged, she returned to the open box and began taking out each piece, testing the weight and weave for suitability. She was nearly ready to give up. Only a few pieces remained, and they all looked to be velvet. "Oh well," she sighed aloud. "You've come this far. You might as well empty the box and re-pack it." A dismal gloom rapidly replaced the sunny spirit of Alexa's revolution. She felt forever doomed to being proper, lest someone not think she was a lady, to be what others wanted her to be. At this rate, she would become more and more stifled by propriety until she grew so lost she would never find herself.

She wanted to cry at the death of her first little revolt. Then, folded flat across the whole bottom of the box, she spied a large piece of brown corduroy. "Oh, Lord," she cried. "Thank you." She took the find as a sign of His approval, and her smile was back in place.

Lifting the treasured piece of material, she quickly replaced the remainder of the fabric, tied the box securely, and returned it to its proper stack.

She hurried downstairs to the small alcove off the sitting room where the treadle sewing machine stood. It hadn't been used since Alexa arrived, but now she took off the lid to reveal a brand-new machine. In one of the cupboards, she found a basket containing threads of many colors, scissors, thimbles, needles, and pins.

Alexa laid the material out on the floor and folded it in half. Another of the skills Aunt Cassy had insisted she learn was sewing. Alexa hadn't been particularly thrilled with the idea, but as usual, had learned in spite of her own desires. Now she was thankful she had.

Without benefit of a pattern, she quickly designed and cut out her riding skirt. Threading the machine, she began sewing the pieces into a gored skirt, split so that when she stood it looked like a normal skirt. When she wanted to ride, though, she could swing her leg over Molly, sit astride, and still be fully covered.

By dinner time Alexa had finished her creation,

pressed it, and laid it across her bed to wear after she had helped with the dishes. She was going horseback riding this afternoon and not around the barnyard, either. Jake could tell her what she needed to know, then she could be on her way to look over her ranch.

Alexa was too excited to eat much, and it was hard to sit while everyone finished eating. Afterward Emmie seemed unusually picky about the clean-up, but at last everything was tidied to her satisfaction, and Alexa felt free to leave.

She rushed to her room and changed into a pale blue cotton blouse with long, full sleeves and her new brown corduroy split skirt. Wearing Uncle Clyde's brown Stetson, she didn't look like anyone she had ever seen. Nevertheless, she was pleased with the combination, and felt like a ranch owner for the first time. Alexa resolved to make more of these skirts. She even considered making jackets or vests to match and ordering some cowboy boots to replace her thin buttoned boots. Might as well go all the way if she was going to break with tradition!

Emmie usually rested after diner, so Alexa, putting on her cowboy hat and leather gloves, tiptoed out of the house and hurried to the barn. Taking a bucket half full of oats and a rope halter, she quickly snared Molly and brought her back to the barnyard. Tying her near the mounting stump, Alexa searched the tack room for a small saddle. There were several to choose from so she took the one with the highest pommel; more to hold on to. She could even lift it. Grabbing a saddle blanket and bridle, she lugged everything out to the horse.

Standing on the stump, she spread and smoothed the sweat-blanket, then tried to hoist the saddle onto Molly's back. Molly kept backing away, and Alexa missed the target each time. Perspiration beaded on her face and rolled down her back where the sun shone hot.

Exasperated, Alexa stormed, "Molly, you stand still, or I'll hit you over the head with this bucket. Hear?"

Something in the tone of her voice must have communicated. Molly stood still and allowed the saddle to be placed on her back. Alexa paused, baffled by the next steps. There were leather and webbed straps everywhere, and she didn't know which went where. She had no idea how to go about fastening the saddle securely enough to mount.

Molly turned her head and looked directly at Alexa. She rolled her eyes and shook her head as if to say, "Go away and leave me alone."

"I am not going away," Alexa retorted. "I intend to learn to saddle and ride you properly."

"Need a little help cinching up the girth, Miss Alexa?" Jake asked as he magically appeared at her elbow.

"If you'd show me how so I can do it by myself, I'd be enormously grateful," she said.

Jake stood eyeing the saddle. "Sure you got the right saddle?"

"I'm sure. I have no intention of riding on that cleverly designed torture device."

Jake shrugged and reached under Molly's belly for the girth, a webbed strap with a ring in the end. Then he made four loops with the leather strap in front of him. "Now make sure the cinch is close to the forelegs, not across the horse's belly," Jake instructed. "Work the cinch tight."

She watched as he kept working out the slack in the leather strap and pulling the cinch tighter and tighter. "Aren't you making it awfully tight?"

"Horse always holds air. Won't be too tight when she starts breathing normal again. In fact, if you was to do some fancy riding and roping you'd have to stop and cinch the saddle tighter." Jake wrapped the strap around the loops of leather and slipped the end through the top ring holding the strap. Then he brought it back through itself, making a fine flat knot.

"There. That's all you do," he said, and patted Molly on the rump.

"If you have time, I'd like to practice."

"You're the boss," Jake reminded her.

She liked the sound of the words and as she undid the saddle, she savored them over and over. After she had saddled the horse several times, she was finally given Jake's blessings. "Always be sure you mount from the left," he warned, for somehow in all the fussing, Molly had turned around and was facing the opposite direction.

Dutifully, Alexa turned Molly and swung into the saddle as she had seen David do. She was now confronted with one small problem. Her feet dangled at the side of the horse nowhere near the stirrups.

Alexa hooked her knee over the saddle horn and gathered her skirts out of his way, while Jake replaced each stirrup until it was the right length. Alexa went walking happily off across the meadow and along a trail into the trees.

Then, she bounced painfully in the saddle. Once on the trail, Molly broke into a trot and Alexa jounced helplessly, and couldn't get Molly to travel at any other gait. Finally, the stitch in her side became so severe, she could hardly breathe. "Molly, whoa!" Molly kept on trotting, heedless of Alexa's command. "Stop, girl," Alexa begged and pulled back hard on the reins. Molly stopped suddenly. If it hadn't been for the high pommel, Alexa would have sailed right over Molly's head. Alexa slipped her feet from the stirrups and slid to the ground. She pressed her side in an attempt to cure the stitch and breathe normally again.

"Well, Miss Spence, you certainly present an arresting sight. One not seen every day out here in the woods.'

She recognized Martin Taylor's voice, but she couldn't see him. "Martin Taylor, where are you? And what do you mean spying on a lady in distress?"

"The lady rode into my territory, although I am forced to qualify the term 'lady.' Never saw a lady riding as you just were." He walked toward her from out of the woods, leading his horse.

Alexa stood, still clutching her side. "I refuse to ride sidesaddle. That is one tenet of being a lady I intend to flaunt. However, I find I don't have as much control as I thought I would."

"Molly's trotting give you a stitch in your side?" he asked, eyeing her hand.

She nodded.

"Bend over," he commanded.

She did but apparently not far enough to suit him for she felt his hand in the middle of her back and then her nose nearly hit the ground as he shoved her roughly. She felt her hat roll off into the dirt. "Ugh!" she gasped breathlessly. Even against her determined struggle to straighten up, his superior weight kept her pinned in a most uncomfortable and undignified position. "Let me up!"she sputtered, her words muffled by her skirt.

"I will in a minute," he answered casually and continued to hold her down.

"Martin Taylor, you let me up this minute!" And she fought against his hand.

As suddenly as he had pushed her down, he released her. Unexpectedly set free from the pressure, she staggered as she stood upright. He reached for her hat and dusted it off. "Strange hat for a lady. Don't see them wearing Stetsons too often," he commented as he handed it to her. "Stitch gone?"

Amazingly enough, it was. "Yes." Then grudgingly, she added, "Thanks."

"What in tarnation made you choose Molly? She's stubborn about staying at a trot, and a killer at that as you learned."

"Ignorance," Alexa replied. But she was wondering why David had chosen Molly for her. If Molly's gait was a well known trot, then David had to know. Of course, he hadn't expected Alexa to take off on her own, either, and Molly had been gentle around the barn yard.

"Come on. If you're determined to learn to ride, and it appears you are, let's go get a decent horse and start you off right."

"If 'right' is to ride round and round a corral, forget it. I've started out to see my ranch, and I intend to accomplish that goal, Mr. Taylor."

"Miss Spence, I asked you earlier to call me Martin. Now, I'm telling you I won't answer to 'Mr. Taylor', so swallow your proper manners or our communication will rapidly cease."

"Of course, Mr. Taylor," she teased. "Please call me Alexa . . . Martin. I'd hate to think our communication might cease."

"I'll ride that plug you're on," he offered, "but we'll have to switch saddles. I don't relish sitting in that straight jacket.

"Not good?"

"Not good. Don't the front of your thighs and hip bones feel sore from bouncing against that high flat pommel."

She felt. They did. Then she blushed. He had spoken frankly in terms not used in mixed company and not excused himself or seemed the slightest bit remorseful. "Martin, you are no gentleman." She hoped her voice was cold enough to give him frost bite.

He finished the final cinch knot on his saddle now resting on Molly. "Alexa, don't up and pull you parlor manners on me. You can't have it both ways. If you want to be treated like a delicate hothouse flower then you have to abide by the rules . . . sidesaddle, parasol, freckle bleaching cream, proper clothing . . .

the lot. You can't suddenly toss away convention and then call it back when it suits you."

She wanted to throw something at him. The beast! His remarks were made the more maddening because he was right. Worse, she found him most disconcerting because he had the courage to put her in her place. Gentlemen never upbraided a lady or engaged her in argument. She hadn't encountered such honesty in an unrelated male and didn't quite know how to deal with it.

He ignored her obvious dilemma, bent over, and made a cradle of his gloved hands. "Here, put your foot in my hands and I'll boost you onto my horse."

She stepped up, grabbed the saddle horn, and struggled up onto a horse that dwarfed Molly. She couldn't get her balance, and began to slip sideways. Martin reached up and gave her leg the needed push to set her straight in the saddle. The urge to rail at him rose in her, but she bit her tongue. He hadn't seemed to take any more notice of his actions than if she had been a boy.

Alexa watched him swing onto Molly and Molly started off at her usual body-wracking trot. Martin jerked her to a stop. "It's time, horse, you learned some manners. Now, you walk or I'll make your life miserable."

"Think she understands you?" Alexa asked.

"I think she's going to test me."

And Molly didn't disappoint him. She returned to that devastating trot, but this time Martin laid into her with spurs. Molly leaped into a gallop, and they disappeared down the trail in a cloud of dust, while Alexa followed at a pleasant comfortable walk on Martin's horse.

She had begun wondering if Molly and Martin were ever coming back when a lathered defeated Molly walked slowly around a bend in the trail. "I've wanted to have a go at this little beast for a long time, but she was always Clyde's favorite. He spoiled her rotten. Got so he couldn't ride her though, and yet he wouldn't let anyone teach her some manners."

"Looks as if she's learned a lesson today," Alexa observed.

"That remains to be seen. How she acts when you get on her will be the test."

"By the way, what's your horse's name?"

"Doesn't have a name," Martin said.

"Doesn't have a name! Why not?"

"I don't give animals names."

Alexa couldn't comprehend. She named everything, including the mouse that continued to evade the trap in the buttery. "Why not?"

"You name something, means its special. Nothing special about an animal. They just die on you, and then you have to get another."

She couldn't see his face, and his back gave her no clue to the emotions running through him. It was clear, though, from the harsh tones of his voice that he had been deeply hurt by the death of a pet and had never gotten over it.

"Martin, I need to rest a few minutes. Could we stop?"

"Probably a good idea. There's a small stream off the trail a few steps This little beast would probably be grateful for a drink."

She followed him through the trees until they arrived at a willow-lined stream. Dismounting, she walked to the water's edge and looked into the shallows where the stream ran as transparent as glass. Along the bottom, many colored stones formed a unique mosaic shadowed by swimming fish. She followed the creek to deeper places where the water, a translucent jade green, flowed slowly before it churned frothy white over miniature craggy rapids. Resting in pools at the foot of a short falls, it turned into subdued indigo blue.

"This is a beautiful spot," she breathed softly.

"This whole place is beautiful," he answered.

"Then why are you so set on destroying it?" she asked, remembering Mrs. Hornbeck's comment.

"I'm not destroying it. I'm not cutting timber anywhere near here."

Alexa would continue this conversation another time. But right now she had stopped for a different reason. Sitting on a fallen log, she watched Martin water the horses. He turned them to graze, then came to sit beside her.

"What kind of pet did you have that died?" she asked softly.

He looked at her. His eyes narrowed and his mouth tightened, showing his displeasure at her abrupt question. "None of your business."

"I know it isn't, but your voice when you spoke of your pet showed how deeply you had cared. Can't you share your sorrow?" Would he answer? She hoped so; it was clear that he still carried grief over a loss she guessed was many years old. A childhood grief that continued to cast a pall over his life even today.

CHAPTER 6

MARTIN REMOVED HIS GLOVES and laid them on the log. Reaching out, he plucked a stem of new growth from a nearby choke cherry bush and began shredding each leaf with intense deliberation. Alexa stared at the destruction, stared at the knife-like fingernail as it sliced open the veins until all the leaves lay in shapeless ruins.

Finally, she broke the silence. "Was it a dog?" she asked gently.

He nodded and again the silence hung heavy between them.

She wondered if she dared ask her next question for it was the one that had brought them to this moment. She decided she had better and get his reaction over with. "What was his name?"

Another long silence. "Tramp," Martin answered at last, his voice barely a whisper as though it had been a very long time since he had said the name.

"How did you get him?"

He plucked another branch and began again the methodical destruction of its leaves. Much later he spoke. "My father was a railroad engineer. The dog was hurt in the train yard and nearly starved to death because he couldn't get food. One day, he followed my father home from work. I was playing in front of the house when they came up the street, a gray short-haired dog limping along behind, and my father trying to get him to go back." Martin stopped and it seemed he wasn't going to continue.

"What happened next?"

"I asked him about the dog. He said that the mutt had attached himself to the train crew, but after he was hurt he was real ugly and boney. Nobody wanted him. My father didn't want him either, but Tramp and I took to each other right off."

Alexa watched and waited as Martin began slowly pacing back and forth through the grass. It was a long time before he spoke again. He seemed to have forgotten her entirely. His pacing created a well-defined path and still he walked.

At last, he returned to the log, took off his hat, and laid it on the grass as he sat down beside her. He ran long, slender fingers through the mop of untamed hair . . . the fingers and hands of a gentleman, not an unmannered logger. Leaning forward, he propped his elbows along his thighs. The hands dropped limply from the wrists and hung, unmoving in mid-air. His deep, sometimes overloud growl was gone when he began to speak, replaced by a quiet and cultivated, satin-smooth bass. "I had a passel of brothers and sisters, and I was kinda lost in the middle somewhere. My mother wasn't very well, and she had a hard time handling all of us. With my father away from home so much, she did what had to be done. Unless you were sick or in trouble, you weren't noticed much. We weren't allowed out of the yard unless it was to run an errand, and nobody was permitted to come play. Ma said she had enough of her own; she didn't need to tend other people's kids. Tramp became my best friend."

Alexa felt a knot of tears rise in her throat. She could picture a lonesome little boy curled up with his dog and she wanted to touch him, let him know someone cared, but she refrained lest he misunderstand.

"Did he sleep with you?"

A quick bitter laugh punctuated his answer. "There wasn't room. We slept three and four to a bed as it was. Sure no place to put a dog, too. I used to get up on summer nights, though, and go lie with Tramp on the back porch." A shy smile at the memory changed the severity of his face. The love for that dog still radiated from Martin like heat from a stove.

"How long did you have him?" Alexa asked.

"Six years."

"What happened?"

Briefly, Martin turned stricken eyes to her, the pupils large and dark. Then he bowed his head so she could see nothing but the profile of his face. In the long interval that followed, she became conscious of cheerful bird calls and the soft happy-sounding splash of the water as it ran past . . . incongruous sonds. The chomping of the horses as they ate grew uncommonly loud in the deathly hush that fell between them.

A very long time passed before he spoke again. She had difficulty recognizing the small broken voice as he choked, "When I was thirteen someone poisoned him."

"Oh, no, why?"

Martin shook his head slowly back and forth. "I don't know," he answered in a whisper, separating and accenting each word. "I tried and tried to figure it out . . . tried to remember if I'd done something to someone so they'd want to get even. Tried to remember if Tramp had been doing things he shouldn't. I just couldn't make any sense of it . . . then or now." He almost looked like that puzzled young boy trying to understand how such a calamity could occur.

Alexa felt the hurt deep inside him. Knew somehow it had been the pivot point of his life when he had ceased to trust anyone or share his private feelings. "What did your parents do?"

He faced her and she looked into deep pools of grief openly revealed in his eyes. "Nothing." The word hung in the air between them, cold and unforgiving.

So this was the bottom of the pit . . . the reason he withdrew from emotions of tenderness, lived the transitory existence of a baudy logger, allowed no permanent relationships. She had known him for very little time, but she had already felt his barbed wire warnings to stay clear of his private territory..

When she recovered her voice, she asked softly, "Why not?"

"Ma was having another baby and Pa was on a run. When he got home and I told him about Tramp, he said 'Good. Glad to be rid of that mangy beast. He was an embarrassment to the family. Get you a good dog, now.' And he did. He brought me home a pedigreed Irish Setter from my aunt's kennel." The empty tone in Martin's voice told her all she needed to know about his relationship with the new dog.

Silent tears spilled down Alexa's face. "Tell me the rest of Tramp's story, please," she said brokenly.

He started to speak, cleared his throat, and tried again. Still nothing came out. He stood up, his back to her, head bowed, and shoulders hunched forward. His thumbs were tucked in his front pockets, something she hadn't noticed him do before. She watched him dig a hole with the toe of his boot. And still he didn't say anything. Was this the thirteen-year-old Martin she was seeing? The forlorn, heartbroken boy re-living agonizing moments alone again?

She couldn't stand his solitary suffering any longer. He'd suffered through Tramp's death by himself the first time. She wasn't going to let him re-live the memory alone even if it meant breaking all the rules in Aunt Cassy's book.

Alexa took off her hat and rose from the log to stand in front of him. Wrapping her arms around his waist, she laid her head against his chest and hugged him to her. "It's all right to cry, Martin. It doesn't make you less a man. It makes you more of a human being." She raised her tear-stained face to his and watched his face knot in emotional anguish. A deep, wrenching sob ripped itself loose from his heart where it had been imprisoned all these years. It brought with it all the lonely hurting and emotional neglect from his childhood . . . the lack of time for affection, the isolation amid numbers of brothers and sisters, the limited understanding of his need for love, and finally the tortured death of the thing he loved most.

Once the dam was broken, Martin crushed her against him and continued to sob harsh cleansing tears. She could feel his hands working, kneading her back until the emotional storm spent itself. At last, he let her go and groped in his pocket for a handkerchief. She found his hand and pulled him down until they sat beside each other on the ground with their backs resting against the log. When he had returned the handkerchief to the pants pocket, she reached over and took his hand again.

"Did you watch Tramp die?"

He nodded. "It was a warm fall night, and I heard him whine underneath the open bedroom window. He hadn't acted that way before so I knew something was wrong. I dressed and tiptoed downstairs."

Alexa could see the muscles working in Martin's jaws. He placed his other hand on top of hers and clasped it close to him.

"When I got to him, his whole body was trembling and he was crying in little yips. He couldn't walk, so I picked him up and carried him over to a vacant lot where his cries of pain wouldn't disturb anyone. Then I sat with him. I didn't know what else to do. He'd drag himself along the ground on his belly trying to ease the pain, then he'd stop and shudder all over. Finally, he grew so weak he just lay with his head in my lap, and I prayed, while we both cried."

Alexa felt his warm tears drop on her hand. She took her handkerchief and gently wiped his cheeks.

"When Tramp had gone, I sat a long time petting him. I couldn't believe my only real friend was dead. Finally, I dug a grave and buried him where he'd died, there in the vacant lot under a big oak tree. I prayed over his grave, and then sat with him until morning."

Shaking again with sobs, Martin took Alexa in his arms as he wept away the last of the too-long harbored grief. Eventually, washed clean of this burden, his breathing returned to normal. He unclasped her and fell back against the log. Seeking and finding her hand, he laced his fingers through hers, closed his eyes, and rested his head on the log. She laid her head on his shoulder, and they quietly sat as the sun passed its zenith and turned the morning to afternoon.

At last, he stirred and looked down at Alexa. "You're very young. Where did you get all that old wisdom?" His eyes, now a soft misty gray, warmed her with their glow. In their depths lay a new peace.

She smiled up at him. "Comes from being a woman."

"Not from any woman I've ever known."

"Have you ever given one a chance to know you?"

"None ever wanted to."

"Sure about that?"

"Very sure."

She had a nearly overwhelming urge to throw her arms around him and hug him, show him how much she cared. But she restrained herself lest he misread the meaning of so rash an act. Besides, she had broken enough rules of decorum for one day.

In an attempt to return to the easy comraderie they had enjoyed earlier, she grabbed at the first thing that crossed her mind. "Do you suppose we'd feel better if we washed our faces in the stream?" she suggested, her voice bright and vigorous.

Without a word, he stood, and pulled her to her feet. Walking to his saddle, he opened one of the bags lashed to the side and took out a towel. "That water runs right off a snow bank. It's going to freeze your freckles," he warned, and flashed her a wide smile that spread creases across his face like pebble-tossed circles over the surface of still water.

"Any chance the freezing would make them drop off?"

"None. Besides I like them. Makes you look less like the perfect doll who arrived in our little valley, and more like a real person." He hung the towel around his neck and knelt beside a quiet pool created where the water ran slow. He reached up a hand to Alexa, and accepting his offer of support, she knelt beside him.

She hadn't taken his warning about the water temperature seriously. However, it took only a few well-placed handfuls to numb both her hands and face and she came up dripping. He met her with the towel and tenderly patted her face and hands dry. Turning, he laid the towel over the log in the sun. "Not smart to pack a wet towel."

Then, he enfolded her in his arms and she clasped her hands around his back. It seemed so natural to stand with him like this—one not leaning on the other, but meeting squarely and equally. She stood, aware of his vitality, and yet he seemed also to recognize and respect her strengths.

At last, she broke the silence between them. "I feel a great desire to pray and give thanks. Will you join me?"

Wordless, they turned and knelt, bowed their heads, and rested their folded hands on the log. "Thank you, Lord, for the peace that has been restored to Martin. Thank you, Lord, for this beautiful world and this perfect spot in it. Thank you for the friendship that Martin and I enjoy. Amen.'' Alexa sensed that Martin, too, wished to pray and so they continued to kneel.

He cleared his throat, then reached for her hand. With hands joined together, he began, ''Lord, I haven't been on my knees as often as I should, but I'd like to change that . . . beginning right now. Thank you for sending Alexa, for I know you did, to cleanse my heart and make it whole again. Thank you for giving me another chance to make something of my life. Amen.''

Then they stood and walked together in peace and tranquility through the meadow, letting the serenity of God fill their souls.

At last, Martin broke the silence. '' I've told you a great deal about my life. I know scarcely anything about yours.''

She smiled into his dappled gray eyes. ''I was thinking how similar our childhoods were. I was orphaned at four and went to live with Aunt Cassy who was no relation at all. Her husband was a salesman and away much of the time. She had only boys and was happy to take me. She had always wanted a little girl and I became the pride of her life. I constantly tried to do her bidding for fear she would send me away if I didn't.''

He interrupted. ''You mean she threatened you.''

''She never even hinted at such a thing. I built the whole thing in my mind because I thought I was completely alone in the world. I didn't know about my Uncle Clyde until just a few years ago when he finally tracked me down. Since he left me all this, I'm finally beginning to learn about the real me buried underneath all the layers of right-doing. I fear I may discover a very rebellious soul if today is an example.''

He laughed. "You think the world will stop spinning because you refuse to ride sidesaddle and wear a poke bonnet? Well, it won't. And you won't be any less a lady. You're very modestly clad and that Stetson looks far more like a rancher than a bonnet. I, for one, approve heartily"

"And I'm grateful for your support. But this isn't getting me a different horse and a riding lesson. Or do you think Molly has learned her lesson and will be good?"

"She may have learned her lesson from me, but you don't have what it takes yet to convince her. Give yourself a little time, then you can show that mule who's boss. Just promise to let me know, though, the day you decide on the lesson."

"I will." Alexa suddenly felt so full of life she couldn't stand to walk, and so she raced off toward the grazing horses as fast as she could run. Martin, in his heavy boots, came pounding after her, caught up, and ran along side until they arrived at the horses.

Her hair, fallen from its pins, streamed down her back as she leaned against a tree gasping for breath. "I look like a wanton woman and I don't have enough pins left to repair the damage," she said, running fingers through the untamed locks.

"Braid it. You still have a few pins. They'll hold the braids." Martin helped locate the few pins that hadn't fallen out completely as the two of them ran. "Here, hold these," he ordered.

She held out her palm, and he dropped his supply of pins into it.

"Turn around." He spoke softly as he took her by the shoulders and pivoted her until her back was to him.

"What are you doing?"

"Braiding your hair." His voice, smooth and casual, warmed her.

She hadn't had her hair braided since she was a

75

young child. Aunt Cassy said braids were common so Alexa had endured endless nights with her hair rolled up in rags to make curls and then painful hours combing the curls into a proper hairdo.

"This isn't going to be a first-rate job since we don't have a comb or a brush, but at least your hair will be up." He worked silently. She could feel him part the hair with his fingers and work the three strands into a single braid that fell to the middle of her back. "You have beautiful hair, thick and sweet-smelling," he said as he finished pinning the braid around her head. He held her away from him and studied the results. "I'm not crazy about that style. I like the braid just hanging down your back, better."

"Very well, since you're the one who has to look at me, let it hang."

He took out the pins and let the rope of russet hair fall down her back. He reached for her hat and set it carefully on her head. Raising a crooked index finger, he tilted her chin until their eyes met and she stood looking into deep, unfathomable pools of light gray mist. She watched as he slowly bent his face over her. Then, she closed her eyes as she felt his lips move on hers, gentle, sweet-tasting. Felt the slight tickle of his beard on the sensitive skin around her mouth. Felt his breath warm on her cheek. Felt his hand on her cheek as he released her lips and held her from him. She embraced his hand, brought it to her lips, and kissed it. Looking into his eyes she saw tears brimming the edges and felt a rising lump in her throat.

Deciding they had both had enough high emotion for one day, she grasped at any topic that would serve to lighten the mood. "Where did you learn to braid hair?"

He seemed greatly relieved not to be plunged into tears again. "When you had as many little sisters as I did, you learned in a hurry. Keep my skills sharp braiding horses tails."

76

She moved away and toward the feeding animals. "Speaking of horses, we still haven't solved the problem of a name for your horse."

"How about Alexa in honor of the lady who wanted him to have one?" Martin's eyes danced as he waited for her rebuttal to his ridiculous suggestion.

She determined to surprise him. "That's a very lovely thought, Martin, and I am deeply appreciative of your thoughtfulness. However, I don't think a 'he' would like a girl's name. If you're determined to honor me, how about Alexander? You could call him Alex for short." There, that should hold Martin for a minute or two, she thought smuggly and continued to eye him with her most innocent look.

"You really think so?" Martin didn't sound too enthusiastic over the name.

"Oh, absolutely. That's a fine name for a splendid horse. Think of the strength of Alexander the Great. It's really captured in your horse."

"Weeelll, all right," he said reluctantly. "If you insist."

"Martin, I don't insist," she objected. "That would be conceited on my part, insisting you name your horse after me. I was only attempting to accede to your wishes. Please feel free to change his name. My feelings won't be hurt a bit. Not even a little bit."

"I may be an insensitive male, but I know that to be a bald-faced lie. You'd be mad as a dunked cat, so Alex it is and Alex it shall remain."

"Actually, as I look at him, I'm not sure he's a fine enough horse to carry the name Alex. Alexander was an emperor, and I think your horse is only worth a king's name. How does King strike you?"

"You'd settle for King and not be mad?"

"Certainly. There's nothing worse than an animal with a name he can't live up to. I feel much better about the name King."

"So do I," Martin said emphatically.

"It's decided then. Come on, King, start getting used to your name," she said as she found a rock and led him to it. Martin stayed near as she climbed up the rock, and slid easily onto King's back.

Molly's memory wasn't too long, and she tried to trot with Martin again. However, he took her on one more gallop down the trail, and when she returned she walked, chastened and proper, behind Alexa and King.

Long shadows slanted across the fenced meadow as Alexa and Martin rode side-by-side. "I'm afraid it's a little late to try to teach me to ride. What do you think?" she asked.

He examined her face carefully. "I don't think you're too old to learn to ride. People older than you do it all the time."

She looked at his poker face and broke into a laugh. "You know what I mean."

He grinned. "I don't want to agree with you because I don't want a special day to end, but unfortunately, you're right. Got a day full of plans for tomorrow?"

"Nothing that can't wait."

"Good. I'll get the crew going and be over. I planned to scout timber this week. You can go with me."

He didn't leave her weak, trembling, giddy the way David did, but she enjoyed being with Martin. "I'd like that. Shall I have Emmie prepare a lunch?"

"Only as long as it's packed with delicacies, and tasty little surprises to whet the jaded appetite." They arrived at the barn, and he helped her down from King and began to change saddles.

"Don't want much, do you?"

"You obviously haven't tasted the cuisine of a logging camp or you wouldn't ask." He tightened the girth around King's belly and grasping the saddle horn, pulled and pushed the saddle to see how it held.

78

Satisfied, he dropped the stirrup into place and patted King's rump.

"I haven't been invited."

He looked surprised. "You mean you'd come?"

"Is there a reason I shouldn't?"

"No. It's just so few ladies find a lumber camp with its rowdy men socially acceptable. But then . . . I keep forgetting you're no lady."

She folded her arms across her chest and stamped her black leather booted foot. "Martin Taylor!"

He laughed, low and easy as he wrapped his arms around her rigid shoulders. "I love it when you get your dander up. Your eyes turn to glittering ice crystals and your jaw sets like granite. You're one dandy woman, Alexa Spence. Real and honest as buttermilk."

She smiled at him, but kept her arms folded. "You make it terribly difficult to be angry."

"I try," he answered, breezily. Looking at the lowering sun, he said, "Get on King, and I'll take you to the house."

Alexa looked at him. "Ride double?"

He settled easily into the saddle and kicked his foot out of the stirrup. "Stand on the stump and I'll help you swing up behind me."

She did as he directed and found it wasn't as hard as it looked. Once on the horse's back and seated on the skirt of the saddle, she grabbed the back of the saddle seat to hold on to. Martin sat back firmly in the saddle and pinned her fingers tight. She felt the blood rush into her face. Worse, she didn't know what to do. What was he thinking, for he surely could feel her hands? What would he think if she moved them? She saw his shoulders begin to shake as he cleared his throat.

"Maybe you could hold on better if you put your hands around my waist."

He leaned forward enough to release her fingers and

after he had settled back, she slid her arms around him. She tried very hard to keep some distance between them, but he was so large and her arms so short, it was impossible. She ended up leaning firmly against him, her cheek against his back.

"That's better," was all he said.

She wondered if this would become a great laugh among the loggers back at the camp. Then she knew he wouldn't share it, anymore than he would the rest of the things that had passed between them this day— this very special day in which they had both moved a bit closer to accepting their pasts.

CHAPTER 7

ALEXA ROSE EARLY AND RUSHED to look out the window. The sky was still a creamy blue along the rim of the mountains as the not yet risen sun diluted an unmarred sky. Martin hadn't said what time he would come for her and she wanted to be ready. This wasn't a day to miss a minute of. *Thank you, God, for another perfect day,* she prayed. *And thank you for the friendship of Martin Taylor. I've never met anyone like him. He doesn't make me all shivery like David does, but he's wonderful to be with and makes me feel I can grow and learn to be myself. Please help him, Lord, to accept himself as the fine person he is. And help me to know how to help Emmie. She's keeping deep secrets and hurts she isn't sharing. Amen.*

After her morning Bible reading and quiet time, Alexa dressed and went into the kitchen where Emmie was busy making breakfast. "Good morning. Anything I can do to help?" she asked.

Emmie gave her a casual glance that turned into a disapproving glare. "You going to wear that heathen costume this morning?" she complained.

"This morning and the rest of the day. And as soon as I can get to town, I'm going to buy some more material and make others. I'll probably wear this or another costume like it most of the time this whole summer," Alexa shot back, keeping her voice even but determined.

"It don't bother you none what the neighbors'll think?"

"Emmie, I don't intend to prance into town dressed like this or go out calling. This skirt is for my own comfort when riding here on the ranch, nothing more."

Emmie's answering "Hummph" let Alexa know she hadn't convinced Emmie of a thing. It didn't matter, though. She liked the feel of the skirt and she planned to wear it.

"Sit down and eat," Emmie ordered and placed a platter of ham and eggs on the table. "The men'll be here in a minute for theirs."

"Good. I need to talk with them," Alexa said as she helped herself to fried eggs fresh from Jake's chickens.

As if they had heard Emmie, the two hands stomped their boots free of dust on the porch and came in through the kitchen. They stopped short when they saw Alexa sitting at the breakfast table. It apparently still bothered them to eat with her.

"Come on and sit down," Alexa invited. "I need some information and advice from you gentlemen. This morning seemed a good time to get it before you're gone and busy."

Bill and Jake hung their hats on the coat rack in the corner and smoothed their hair as they walked to the table. Jake didn't have any problem, for he had only a salt and pepper fringe around a scrubbed bald head. Bill's was another matter, however. He had a fine head of wiry brown hair that refused to be tamed under anything less than his hat.

They pulled up chairs at the far end of the table, leaving a considerable distance between themselves and Alexa. She felt like a reigning potentate from her place at the head of the table, but it was useless to ask them to move closer. They had shut up like clams, and she would not get a word out of either of them.

"How are things with the cattle?" she asked Bill.

"A real good crop of spring calves now I got 'em rounded up and moved where I could count 'em. Need to get 'em branded before they go on the public range, though.

"What do you need to do that?"

"A couple more hands. Jake can tend the fire. Get 'em in. Won't take more'n two, maybe three days." Bill continued to eat, not letting the conversation interfere with his meal.

Apparently the two had talked this over earlier for Jake nodded his agreement.

"You'll need a cook for the bunkhouse, then," she said.

"Cookin' ain't a full-time job for a crew that size. Get three hands. One can cook and work, too" Bill said.

"Very well. Will you see to it?"

"Beggin' your pardon, ma'am, but I already have."

Alexa leaned forward, her forearms resting on the table. "Bill, I don't intend faulting you for your actions. You know what needs doing and I don't. In the future, though, I feel we need to talk each day about the ranch. You can teach me what running a ranch takes. I want to know."

Bill's face turned red. Alexa couldn't tell if it was from her mild reprimand over his taking actions not discussed with her, or if he didn't think a woman had any place in the man's world of ranching. She didn't much care. This was her ranch and she was going to learn about it, from the finances that the banker in town had explained to her, down to the smallest detail of the working day.

"When do you plan to cut the meadow hay?" she asked, changing the subject.

"Middle of July. Looks like a good crop this year." There seemed to be a new respect in Bill's voice. "We'll need extra help then, too."

"Can you keep the men you hire for branding busy until then? Seems a shame to find some good men and then have to hunt for more in a month."

"Got a lot of fence needs fencing. 'Specially over in the woods between us and the loggin' outfit."

"Mr. Taylor assured me he had taken care of that section. Has he not done as he said?"

"It's not that he ain't done anything. Loggers don't fix fences. They just prop 'em up."

"You're saying it's not a permanent repair job."

"Yes'm."

"Very well, then. Let's keep the branding crew if you can find enough for them to do. Now, what time of day is most convenient for you to inform me of the day's accomplishments and what work will need to be done in the future?"

Bill's whole posture altered during this exchange with Alexa. He sat straighter in his chair and gave her his full attention. His voice lost its slightly patronizing edge, and he spoke as employee to employer. "Evenin's when we get through supper, if that's agreeable with you."

"Fine." Alexa turned to Jake. "Are you able to milk a cow?"

He looked startled, then brought up his hands and flexed the thick, calloused fingers. "I could probably get the milk out."

"You don't have arthritis in your hands?"

"No, ma'am. Just ma'knees and most days its not too bad. Gets worse with the cold and damp."

"Would you object to the added chore of milking a cow? I am used to fresh milk and dairy products. Emmie knows how to make cheese and I understand

84

berry season isn't too far away. Cream would turn them into a great treat."

"When you point out all the virtues, I'd be a sorry man to refuse. Gotta tell you, though, been trying for years to sell Clyde on getting a cow. He always felt that was beneath a rancher. Warn't no dairy herd gonna eat up his meadow, he'd say."

My goodness, Alexa thought, *Jake hadn't spoken that many words total to her since she came.* "If he felt that way, how do you happen to have chickens. Doesn't seem he'd have wanted them around either."

Jake's face creased with a little smile accompanied by a cracked chuckle. "I bought me a couple little hens and kept 'em real quiet while Clyde enjoyed fresh eggs for breakfast. By the time he found the hens, he was hooked. Had chickens ever since."

Alexa and Bill laughed aloud and Jake looked proud of himself. "You're a sneaky fellow. Bill, we'd better watch out for him," Alexa said.

Bill gave Jake a fond look. "That man can have anything I have if he gets me thick fresh cream for my coffee."

"And I'll be eternally thankful if I can have some fresh cold milk and butter."

"I'll find us a cow, new freshened. Today if I can."

"Today would be good, because I'll have that branding crew hired and ready to work by Friday," Bill reminded him.

Alexa, scarcely able to contain her delight at the change in the men's attitude toward her, pushed back her chair, indicating they were free to leave. "I don't believe we'll need to talk this evening, do you?" she said to Bill as the men stood.

"Not unless something unexpected comes up. I'll come to you anytime, in that case."

"Thank you, both, very much. I'll alert Emmie to be prepared to take care of the milk, Jake, and tomorrow I'll stock the bunkhouse with food."

85

As Alexa stacked the dishes and cleaned off the table, she could hear Emmie in the kitchen preparing the basket lunch. She had not known how to take Martin's statement concerning logging camp food, but she quoted his comments about delicacies to Emmie. She apparently knew more than Alexa for she started planning immediately how to produce tasty delights to tease Martin's palate.

Emmie set the picnic basket in the buttery to stay cool and went on about her work. Alexa spent the time waiting for Martin by sewing straps to her hat, so she could slip it off her head and still keep track of it. She had no intention of wearing it semi-permanently attached as did the men, only doffing it briefly in the presence of a lady and removing it the last thing before their heads touched the pillow at night.

It was shortly before ten when Martin rode up and tied his horse to the new hitching post. Alexa debated if she should wait until he knocked, but decided that was for beaux coming to call. Martin certainly didn't fit in that category so she ran out to meet him.

"Good morning," she called as he finished tying King.

"'Morning. See King's had his last nibble of your hollihocks," Martin said as he patted the hitching post.

"I hope so. He made a real meal the last time he was here." She pointed to a section of well-cropped flowers struggling with new growth.

Martin gave the plants a cursory glance as he walked up the steps to join her. "Ready?"

"As soon as I get my hat and gloves, and the lunch basket."

"Lunch basket! You mean 'basket' as in . . . big basket?" He made a shape in the air with his hands approximately the size of the one Emmie had packed.

"Yes," she said, puzzled at his emphasis.

"Have you thought how you're going to transport it? Pack mule, maybe?"

She hadn't thought and Emmie obviously hadn't either. She looked at him, speechless.

"Then, may I suggest we find you a horse, grab a couple of quick sandwiches for the saddle bags, and save the basket until we get back. Maybe take it down by the creek for our supper?" He cocked his head and waited for her decision.

She smiled and nodded. "Sounds like a most diplomatic solution. However, let's prepare the food and take it to the barn with us."

"Fine with me," he said and opened the door for her to enter the house.

Emmie was out in the garden so Alexa prepared cold sliced beef sandwiches and some oatmeal and raisin cookies, wrapped them in paper and tied the packages with string. Martin lounged against the corner of one of the cupboards, watching her and munching on cookies while he waited.

"You look right at home in the kitchen," he commented.

"I've spent a lot of time in one, but thanks to Emmie or someone like her, I don't plan to in the future." Alexa spoke most emphatically, not leaving any doubt as to her new role.

"Well, then Rancher Spence, let's be on our way."

They went out the kitchen door and walked along the porch to where King stood, patiently waiting. Martin packed their noon meal in his saddle bag, unfastened the reins, and swung into the saddle. Riding King to the foot of the steps where Alexa waited, he stretched out his hand. "Ready?" he asked, his eyes dancing as he looked at her.

She knew what he was thinking and couldn't help blushing. All she did was nod, though. The blush was all the recognition he was going to get of the saddle seat incident last night. She placed her foot in the stirrup and she could feel the strength in his hand and arm as he swept her up behind him. This time he didn't let go of her hand so quickly, and she adjusted her balance before wrapping her arms around his waist.

He turned his head and squinted over his shoulder at her. "Settled?"

"Settled."

She looked down and noticed he gave King the signal to start with a slight pressure of his legs. The horse moved off at the comfortable walk she had enjoyed yesterday. She could have relaxed her grip around Martin and been perfectly safe, but there was a feeling of strength and confidence she gained from the close contact.

Again she watched him signal King with his legs and the horse stopped almost instantly. Martin brought his right leg out of the stirrup, over the front of the saddle, and slid to the ground. He raised his arms to take her from the horse and she beheld his loving face. The soft, gentle look she saw there surprised her. The suspicious narrowing of his eyes and slightly cynical twist to the mouth were gone, replaced by wide-open frankness framed by thick black eyelashes.

"Martin Taylor, it's not fair for a man to have such beautiful long eyelashes. I know women who would kill for lashes like those," she said as she leaned over and placed her hands on his shoulders. His only answer was to smile, wide and relaxed, and she felt his hands close around her waist as he lifted her from King's back.

Her feet securely on the ground, Alexa started to step away, but he continued his grip on her waist. She tipped her face up and met dancing gray eyes. He looked her face over thoroughly. "I'm relieved to see I have no worry in your presence. Your lashes are at least as long as mine. They don't look it, though, because they are lighter auburn at the tips." He took her chin in his hand and moved her head from side to side. "Don't seem to have grown any new freckles since yesterday."

"How could you possibly tell? My face is one continuous freckle."

"I know, but I can tell. Did you have so many when you arrived? I don't seem to remember them."

"By using all manner of creams and a bit of powder, I fooled nearly everyone into believing I had a flawless complexion. It was a lot of work and sacrifice to keep up the masquerade. I'm not willing any more. He who doesn't like my freckles, doesn't like me."

He laughed and hugged her to himself. "I like all of you very much."

They stepped apart and after procurring a halter and some oats, went to select Alexa a horse. They found Jake in the field where the horses were grazing, saddling his horse.

"'Morning, Jake," Martin said. "I've been keeping my eye out for you. You know this stock better than anyone. Which would be a good horse for Miss Alexa?"

Jake returned Martin's greeting with a black glare, completely unlike the warm cooperation he had shown around David. She wondered why and made a mental note to ask him about it when they were alone.

Jake turned to her. "Didn't like Molly, huh?"

"She was wonderful in the corral and around the barn yard. On the trail, it was a different story."

"She needs a strong hand to show her who's boss. Then, she'll be a good horse again," Jake answered.

Alexa thought it wise not to tell him about Martin's already having given Molly her first lessons. "I want a horse with a smooth gait, and one who will mind," she said.

"Got plenty here with a good gait, but ain't no horse gonna mind 'til they know you're boss," Jake informed her.

Rather like a couple of hands I know, Alexa thought. "That's the lesson I hope to learn today," was all she said.

"Well, then. That red roan gelding over there is as good a horse as there is. A might frisky. Ain't been rode this spring. Get him wore down, and he'll be fine."

While she and Jake talked, Martin snared the horse and brought him to her. "Horse got a name?" he asked Jake.

Alexa's heart leaped at the question. *Thank you, Lord, for bringing Martin so far from his hurtful past, so quickly.*

"I call him Red," Jake answered brusquely before he mounted his horse. Turning to Alexa, he said, "I'm off to see about a cow."

She wished him good luck, and he rode off toward town.

She started to take the oat bucket from Martin, but he handed her the halter rope instead. "He's your horse. Better start right now to let him know that. Jake was right when he said the best horse can be rotten if he finds out he's the boss and not you."

Martin handed her the halter rope and walked beside her as she led Red along. He made no further mention of Jake, but was sure he had noticed Jake's cool treatment. Apparently he didn't plan to make any more of it. David's hostility toward Martin, and now Jake's, continued to puzzle her and she fretted over it as they walked back to the barn. What was he doing that would make two such different men react in such a similar way.

When they arrived at the barn, Martin checked Red's feet. "Jake does a good shoeing job," he said, then disappeared into the barn to choose a saddle and bring it out. "This is a twenty-five pound saddle, but can't find one any lighter that's fit to ride. And, the seat's higher in the back than most. It'll give you good support."

"I'm much more interested in the saddle horn. I want something to grip if things start to get out of hand," she said, eyeing the leather-wrapped flat-topped knob.

"Got a good horn," he said, grinning at her.

Red was a good-sized horse so she led him over to the stump. Martin said nothing as Alexa took the saddle blanket from him and laid it over Red's back and smoothed out the wrinkles. She hefted the saddle. For being a fourth of her weight, it wasn't as bad as she had expected. It was bulky and awkward to handle, but she grabbed it, front and back. Stepping up on the stump, she gave it a swing and plumped it down squarely in the middle of Red's back.

"Not bad," Martin commented.

"What do you mean, 'not bad'? That was perfect," Alexa announced, pleased with herself for having succeeded on the first try. She set about tightening the double cinches while Martin watched every move she made. She finished the final knot and gave Red a slap on the rump as she had seen Jake do.

Martin squinted at her from under the wide brim of his hat. "Where'd you learn to saddle a horse?"

His voice held an astonishment that pleased Alexa no end. "I could lie and tell you I've been doing it for years, or say that Jake taught me yesterday."

"He did a good job teaching you."

"On the contrary," she retorted as she slipped the bit into Red's mouth. "I did a great job of learning."

"A little success went right to your head, I see," he commented dryly, and double checked the tightness of her saddle.

She laughed, slightly embarrassed. "I received so little praise from Aunt Cassy, no matter how hard I tried to accomplish something, that I took to praising myself silently. Then I didn't feel so bad at not achieving to her expectations. My little pat on the back slipped out. You weren't supposed to hear it."

He put his arm around her shoulder and hugged her to him. "We both had it kinda rough, didn't we?"

"We did, but look at the character it developed."

"Did you say . . . characters?"

They both laughed, leaned a moment together as another strand was added to the bond between them, then they separated to mount their horses.

"I'll set your stirrup length after you get on," he said.

The stirrups were so long, she had a little trouble swinging into the saddle. Then she hooked her left leg around the horn while he re-laced the stirrup. Shortening stirrups was a tedious job and when it was finished, the saddle would become hers by virtue of the stirrup length.

At last, Martin was satisfied. "Stand in 'em," he ordered.

"You mean, literally?"

"I do."

She put the stirrups on the balls of her feet and stood. She cleared the saddle seat by about three inches.

"You need to ride with your feet like they are now. Also, if we move faster than a walk you can do what's called posting. You stand and move with the gait of the horse," he instructed.

"You don't ride that way," she objected.

"I've also been riding for years."

"Did you start by riding that way?"

"No," he confessed.

"Then, I don't intend to either," she announced and sat back on the seat.

"You are one stubborn woman, Alexa Spence." But admiration rang in his voice, and she took his remark as a compliment. "I know you don't want to ride around the corral today, but Red's been roaming all spring. It's always wise to test your horse before you get too far from home. Check first to see if he'll rein from the neck."

She laid the rein against his neck and he turned his head the opposite way.

"Good. Now, get him started."

She remembered the way Martin signaled King, and tightened her knees against Red's side. He moved into a brisk walk. She reined his neck and he turned back. Pressing her knees into his sides, he stopped. She reached down and patted his neck. "You are going to be a fine horse."

Martin rode up beside her and showed her how to hold the reins. She slipped the reins between her fingers as he demonstrated, and started off at a brisk trot. She was bouncing all over the place again, and she reined Red to a stop.

"That, my dear, is why you post when you can't sit the saddle," he said quietly.

"You're sitting your saddle and you're not posting. What are you doing differently?" she demanded to know.

"I'm not trotting my horse, for one thing. I don't care a lot about riding that gait. If you don't either, move him into a canter. It's a bit faster and a lot smoother. Then, sit back firm in the saddle and relax. Get the feel of your horse and go with it."

They started again and she moved Red quickly into the canter. Martin was right. This was a lovely gait and she concentrated on doing as he had instructed. She pushed firmly into the saddle and tried to go with the horse. Soon, she had the feel of him and urged him into a gallop. It was stimulating to feel Red's powerful rippling muscles propelling her forward at such a rate. The wind rushed against her face and through her hair as she flew along. She felt transported to another place and time. A place where nothing could suppress her great spirit and it rose, free at last, to fill all space and time in the enchanted land. Riding horseback was the grandest thing she had ever done.

CHAPTER 8

"You bin hunched over them ledgers all morning. It's time you took a stretch," Emmie ordered, as she entered Alexa's bedroom and set a small plate of cookies and a glass of milk on the rolltop desk next to her. "You're gonna be so stiff from your ride yesterday, you won't move normal for a week."

"You're too late. I didn't know I had so many different muscles in my body, and everyone of them objecting to their treatment," Alexa said, bracing her hands on top of the desk and pushing herself to a standing position.

Emmie sniffed and retreated to the doorway. "I don't wonder, galloping around like a wild schoolboy. You'll get no sympathy from me."

Alexa gritted her teeth and turned to walk toward Emmie. She bit back the moan that threatened to escape as the abused and over-worked muscles screamed their distress at the treatment they'd received. "How long am I going to be like this?" she asked when she could speak.

"A good long time if you don't get some exercise," Emmie said.

94

Alexa took a step and gasped at the amount of pain it caused. "Exercise! I can hardly move."

Emmie shrugged. "Up to you. You're the boss. Got plenty of people to wait on you until you recover." She moved toward the bed with its tall handcarved, oak headboard. "Want me to turn your covers down?"

Alexa eyed the bed with longing. She knew Emmie was right. If she crawled between the covers of the inviting feather bed, she would probably turn into a stick of wood and never walk again, much less get on a horse. "What sort of exercise do you recommend?"

"While it will pain you greatly at first, the best kind is getting back on that horse." Emmie stood unbending, her arms folded across her body, allowing no pity for Alexa to escape. "Might try the sidesaddle this time," she needled.

That did it. "Never!" Alexa stormed. "I'll ride my western saddle until I die or it kills me. At the moment either option seems imminent and can't occur too soon." Her storm ended in a pitiful whimper.

Emmie dropped her arms and peered closely into Alexa's face. "Face looks a mite pale and pinched. Hurt that bad?"

Alexa drew a deep, rugged breath. "Hurts worse," she said as she hobbled slowly toward the door, groaning inwardly with each step.

In the next moment, Emmie's arm descended around Alexa's shoulder and she mopped the perspiration beading on Alexa's upper lip and forehead as she continued the tortuous way down the hall.

"I'll make you some catnip tea. Help the pain a bit, but the only real cure is to get back on your horse."

At the thought of hauling herself on top of Red, Alexa could hardly keep back the tears. In fact, the thought of walking to the barn and then out to catch him in the pasture was enough to make her whole body scream.

Alexa eased into a chair and watched Emmie dip water from the bucket standing near the sink into a small tin copper-bottomed tea kettle and set it on the stove. "Was your day yesterday worth this?" she asked as she prepared the herbs in a cup.

For the first time this morning, Alexa smiled. "Yes, Emmie, it most definitely was. We rode through the big timber at the back of my place. I've never seen trees like that. Cedars a thousand years old, hemlock, and Douglas fir. And acres of white pine. The ground underneath was covered with different types of ferns growing thick and high." She paused in reflection before continuing. "There was an undisturbed solitude that made one feel holy." Nodding slowly, she concluded, "Yes, it truly was worth today's misery."

"Glad it makes your pain bearable. Bin a shame to suffer for nothing." Emmie set the teacup in front of her. "Let it steep awhile longer 'fore you drink it."

"I didn't tell you, but Martin said you can come cook for his crew any time. In fact, he might even try to hire you away from me."

Emmie, standing at the stove, looked back over her shoulder disapprovingly at Alexa. "I may be desperate someday, but not that desperate. Cooking for a bawdy logging crew is more'n even I can stomach."

"Are they that bad?" Alexa tried to imagine Martin, strong and determined when the occasion called for it, but gentle and tender underneath, behaving as she had heard loggers did—then drinking and womanizing his money away after a long day's work.

"Worse!" and she refused to discuss the subject further.

Alexa drank her tea and, deciding to take Emmie's advice, put on her hat and gloves and hobbled to the barn. The walk, slow and pain-wracked, took a great deal of determination. By the time she caught Red and saddled him, she wondered if Emmie wasn't right and she had lost any good sense she had ever had.

Standing on the stump, she slipped her foot in the stirrup and started to swing her right leg over the horse. The pain that shot through her brought tears and a cry she couldn't contain. As she sat astride Red trying to regain a bit of composure, Jake came hurrying out of the barn.

"You all right, Ma'am?" he asked, worry creasing his forehead above a hawklike nose and faded blue eyes.

"I'm not, but there's nothing you can do about it," she said, her voice still trembling slightly from the effect of the stabbing pains.

A smile of understanding crossed Jake's face replacing the tense concern. "Overdid the riding a mite yesterday?"

"You're welcome to call it 'a mite'. I'd refer to it as greatly overdone. Emmie, however, tells me this is the best way to undo the damage." Alexa shifted her position in the saddle in an attempt to relieve the throbbing ache.

"She's right. Ride awhile, then get off and walk. Take you about a week to work all the stiffness out."

"A week! Are you serious?"

"Won't hurt like it does now. Even be better by this afternoon if you'll do what I say. You'll feel less and less sore each day. Be stiff when you get out of bed in the morning, for a spell, but a few hours in the saddle'll ease it right away. But here I stand ajawin', takin' up yer ridin' time."

He whacked Red across the rump and Alexa trotted out of the barnyard. She immediately slowed Red to a walk, regained her breath, and rode off toward the woods.

Alexa found Emmie bent nearly double with her head inside a cupboard when she returned late in the afternoon. Emmie straightened quickly at the sounds of Alexa opening the door and crossed to her immediately. "Land, girl, I didn't mean you was to put in another full day on the back of that horse," she said as Alexa limped through the kitchen door. "You ain't even had a bit to eat since breakfast."

"I'm not hungry," Alexa said.

"I got some water hot in the bath. A good soak should relax you, then some food and a nap. Make you feel a heap better." All the while she talked, Emmie led Alexa across the hall to the bathroom.

While Alexa removed her clothes, Emmie prepared the bath. "You get in and heat it up gradual. Make it as hot as you can stand."

After Emmie left, Alexa hung her white muslin robe on the back of the door and stepped into the warm water. She poured in hot water until she felt sure she would come out boiled, and lay back to soak. She must have dozed off, for the timid knock on the door startled her.

"You still in there?" Emmie said softly.

"Yes, Emmie, but I'm getting out right now."

"There's a cowhand here from Mr. Hornbeck's ranch. He's got a letter for you."

Alexa's heart took a great leap. David! "I'll be decent in a minute," she answered and, ignoring the still stiff muscles, vigorously toweled herself dry. Wrapping up in the robe, she opened the door slightly.

Emmie handed Alexa the letter through the crack. "He's waiting for an answer," Emmie said.

"Thank you. I'll hurry." Alexa tore open the heavy cream colored envelope and removed the letter. She read the well-formed masculine script.

Dear Alexa,

If it is agreeable, I would very much like to come calling this evening about eight. I find I am unable to wait to see you until Mother comes to visit on Tuesday.

Your obedient servant,

David Hornbeck

Alexa rushed to her roll-top desk near the front door of the bedroom, praying all the while that her hand would stop shaking enough to answer his request properly. She found some suitable white linen paper trimmed with a small gold border and quickly assured David that she would be delighted to have him call this evening. Folding it, she slipped the note into a matching envelope and sealed it.

Alexa opened the door enough to hand Emmie the letter.

Dashing back to the bathroom, she knelt beside the tub and poured water through her hair to wet it.

"Child, what are you doing in there?" Emmie called through the door.

"Washing my hair." Keeping her eyes squeezed shut against the dripping water, Alexa fumbled for the towel.

"Washing your hair! With that stock you have, it'll never be dry by midnight, much less before Mister David comes." Emmie sounded thoroughly vexed.

Alexa wrapped her head in a towel, turban-style, and rushed across the hall into the kitchen where Emmie had just finished setting out a meal. "You didn't have to prepare something special for me. I could have waited until supper," Alexa objected.

"I suppose you could have, but you need a nap and time to dress proper for Mr. David. And now, time to dry and curl your hair." Emmie gave Alexa a pinch-mouthed look of disapproval. "Wait for supper and you'll be rushed." Emmie set the bowl of stew in front of Alexa as she sat at the small work table in the kitchen.

Alexa stared up at Emmie. "How did you know what was in the letter?"

Emmie jammed her hands into her apron pockets and rocked back slightly on her heels, a smug look spread all over her face. "It don't take a lot to guess. Way that young fella looks at you is hint enough.

Knew he'd never be able to go 'til Tuesday without seein' ya. And if he hadn't come here, I'm guessing you'd a figured a way to go there."

"Emmie!" Alexa protested, shock at the suggestion vibrating through her voice. "I would never do such a thing."

"We won't know, will we? Since Mr. Hornbeck's so obliging and saved you the trouble of cooking up a scheme."

Before Alexa could raise further objections, Emmie disappeared through the door. It pained Alexa to admit it, but Emmie was right. She had been thinking about David all afternoon and wondering if she was going to be able to go until Tuesday without seeing him.

Her stew finished, she walked to her bedroom, noting as she went how much less stiff and sore she was. Thank goodness for people like Emmie and Jake. Emmie had the bed turned down and Alexa longed to slide between the cool white sheets. But she had to dry her hair first.

Alexa went out on the porch where the sun and warm breeze would dry her hair quickly. Then she braided the rust-colored tresses loosely in single rope down her back, which reminded her of Martin's gentle touch. Through a drowsy fog, she tried to imagine David Hornbeck braiding a woman's hair, but she couldn't conjure up a picture of him performing such a service. Sometime during this musing, she sank into a renewing sleep and dreamed that David read her poetry while Martin braided her hair.

A soft tapping on her door wakened Alexa. "Yes," she answered, her voice filled with sleep.

"Time to wake up if you don't want to hurry in your preparations for Mister David," Emmie said.

"Thanks, Emmie." Alexa rolled over slowly and found as she moved, the tightness in her muscles was much improved.

Throwing back the covers to let the bed air, she stood and did some slow stretching moves. It was truly amazing how well she felt. She crossed the royal blue, flowered carpet to the large wardrobe standing against the bathroom. Opening it, she removed several dresses, but decided they were too formal. She didn't want to appear too eager so she chose a heliotrope, chambray shirtwaist with large bishop sleeves and a double ruffle down the front and back. The heat of the day seemed to be lingering, so she decided on a black poplin skirt with four inch knife pleats around the bottom. The three rows of white braid trimmed the pleats.

Over her white muslin drawers and chemise, she placed a proper corset. Just as she prepared to call Emmie, a knock sounded at the door. "You need me to help you lace your corset?"

"Come in. I would swear you have a gift. I was just going to call you," Alexa said.

"I'm glad to see you're going to look like a lady again," was Emmie's only comment as she tightened the corset laces.

"Oh, Emmie, that hurts! Please don't lace me so tight."

However, Emmie ignored Alexa's complaints and continued to cinch her tightly into the steel ribbed, satin covered undergarment. "You been running loose too long. You'll forget how a lady dresses," Emmie scolded. "Where's your corset cover and underskirt?"

Alexa nodded toward the oak dresser. "Middle drawer."

Emmie chose a set and helped Alexa slip them on, tying and buttoning them. "You do have dainty garments," she said wistfully as she eyed the luxurious lace trimmings at the bottom of the skirt and around the neck of the corset cover.

"With your first pay, you should buy some trim and cambric and we'll make you some," Alexa suggested.

"That would be nice. Luke'd like that a lot."

"And how will Luke know what kind of underthings you're wearing?"

Emmie looked a bit flustered and her face turned a bright pink. "I write him," she confessed. "He wants to know everything about me, he says. Wants me to tell him little personal things. Says it don't make jail so hard if I do."

Alexa slipped into a pair of black low-cut shoes and then put on her shirtwaist and skirt. She stood admiring herself in the mirror.

"Heliotrope brings out the color of your eyes," Emmie remarked. "Now, if you'll set down, I'll twist up your hair." Armed with brush, comb, and hair pins, she soon had Alexa's hair combed into bangs in the front while the rest was curled and pinned securely high on her head. Emmie stepped back to admire her work. "You look like a real lady. Now mind your manners and you'll fool Mister David completely," she said dryly.

Alexa fastened her timepiece with its elaborately engraved gold case around her neck and inspected the time. It was ten minutes to eight. She checked the turned down collar of her shirtwaist and ran her hand up the back of her head. Everything seemed to be in order. Looking in the mirror, she gave her cheeks a quick pinch to bring up a bit more color. Dabbing a few drops of perfume on her wrists and handkerchief, she mentally declared herself ready to receive Mr. David Hornbeck.

CHAPTER 9

ALEXA STEPPED FROM THE BEDROOM and crossed the hall to the parlor. Emmie had lit the lamps, and their soft light gave the room a serene glow until it reached the chandelier. There it drew life from the multi-faceted crystals and sparkled and danced about the room like a flirtatious debutante. Alexa busied herself fluffing the pillows on the couch and re-arranging them in an attempt to ease her nervousness. The other times she and David had spent alone had been informal, but this was different. It was a formal call, and she knew he expected her to act the part. Lost in her thoughts and fears, she jumped as the clock struck eight. With hands grown cold under the tension, she flipped open the cover on her timepiece. The two clocks agreed. She wanted desperately to lift the curtain and peer out, but manners forbade. If David should be arriving and see her, he could easily conclude she awaited his arrival with great eagerness. While she did, it would be gauche for her to give such a broad hint.

Looking about for something to occupy herself

while she waited, she noticed a thin book lying on a lamp table. Picking up the leather-bound volume of Elizabeth Barrett Browning's poetry, Alexa perched on a small, maroon velvet chair facing the door. Taking great care, she spread her skirts and placed her feet flat on the floor with the heel of one foot nestled in the arch of the other. Icy fingers opened the book cover and turned the pages. Her eyes briefly scanned the pages until she came to Sonnet 43. Here it seemed was what she had unconsciously been searching out. "How do I love thee? Let me count the ways . . . " Although attempting to read, her eyes refused to focus further on the words. David's face replaced the print, and she became lost in the remembrance of his kiss and the imprint of his lips in the palm of her hand.

The knock on the front door startled her. She was so adrift in her memories, she had even failed to hear the hoofbeats of his horse. Careful to return the volume to its place, she stood, smoothing the gored skirt over firm hips. Reassured that everything was in order, she proceeded to the front door, taking the small quick steps society proclaimed most ladylike.

Before opening the door, she took a deep breath to calm herself. If thoughts of David could turn her into a witness ninny, she didn't dare think what actually seeing him might do. She let her hand run one last check on her hair. Why was she stalling? Was she afraid he wasn't so wonderful as she remembered? Could that be it? Would she rather have her memories than face the real man? *Alexa, open that door before he turns around and leaves.*

Straightening her shoulders and lifting her chin, Alexa grabbed the doorknob and jerked open the door. Leaning casually against the frame, David stood grinning at her. "I began to wonder if you'd received my letter. Thought maybe my cowhand had returned with a forgery."

His voice flowed over her like warm honey and she felt her knees grow watery with the realness of him. She needn't have worried about his looks. He was even more handsome than she remembered. She found everything about him appealing — from the dark brown hat sitting low over his eyes, to the bronze-tanned skin pulled taut across his high cheek bones, his flawless mustache, and the full, softly smiling, lips.

Beaming him a smile of welcome because she felt unable to trust her voice, she stepped back into the hall and gestured for him to enter. The effects of the languid movement of his arm as he removed his hat, the effortless flow of his body as he pushed away from his position against the door jamb and stepped into the hallway, left her straining for breath. His eyes never left her, but moved unhurriedly over her face, stopped at each feature as though memorizing its quality and placement, lingered on her mouth and grew misty at the memories.

Emmie had laced her corset impossibly tight. Alexa decided this was the cause of her breathing trouble.

"I'm pleased you were free to receive me this evening," he said at last, his voice, a smooth cultivated baritone without a trace of western twang.

"I'm delighted that you were free to come," she answered in a voice breathless with anticipation.

His cerulian eyes narrowed slightly and he ran a finger around the celuloid turn-down collar. "I wasn't free," he said, his eyes leaving her face and traveling slowly, taking time to absorb each detail of her throat, the ruffled shirtwaist, the tiny waist corseted to an enviable eighteen inches. "I couldn't stand not seeing you until Tuesday."

His words, spoken soft and intimate against her cheek as he took her hand and tucked it into the bend of her arm, scrambled her senses badly and only by using the greatest determination was she able to force herself to respond in a way resembling proper behavior.

"Tuesday is a long way off," she agreed as they strolled into the parlor.

Sitting on the couch, he took her hand from his arm and held it in his firm grasp, thus making sure they sat close together. She could feel him next to her, feel the hard muscles of his arm flex through his wool tweed suit jacket as her arm lay against his. He laid his hat on the couch and turned to look at her.

Running a finger over her face, he said, "I hope you'll forgive me, but I don't seem to remember so many freckles. They make the blue of your eyes much more intense. I like them."

"That's very kind of you to say. The sun here seems just the right strength to grow a splendid crop."

'I've also noticed your tendency to go about in the sun bare-headed."

"An open act of defiance, I'm sorry to say. Aunt Cassy insisted I wear a poke bonnet at all times. I grew tired of viewing the world from such a narrow perspective."

He laughed. "I approve of your defiance in that regard. I shall encourage you to other such acts."

This seemed a good opportunity to feel him out about her horseback riding. "Would you support my riding a western saddle rather than the sidesaddle you so thoughtfully provided?"

"Perhaps I should have added, within reason."

"I take it you don't feel riding astride is ladylike?"

"Not only is it not ladylike, it could be downright dangerous."

"Dangerous? How so?"

He tensed and his face turned dark red under the tan. "It's not a topic one usually discusses on the first formal call," he said.

Alexa felt terribly slow-witted, but she couldn't for the life of her interpret his line of thinking. "Perhaps I should ask Emmie?"

He sighed audibly. "Yes, I think that would be an excellent idea. I'm sure she can elucidate my meaning."

She felt the tension drain from him and he relaxed against her again. "Tell me about yourself," she urged wanting desperately to change the subject. "You obviously aren't from the west originally. How do you happen to be here in Idaho?"

He toyed with her fingers, rubbing the backs of them with his thumb while he thought. "I'm not trying to avoid your question. It's just, I don't know where to start."

"Have you thought about the beginning?"

"That far back?"

"It obviously had a great effect on your being here this evening," she reminded him.

He looked at her and chuckled. "I can't argue with that. All right," he launched. "I was born in Boston, attended prep schools, and graduated from Harvard."

Harvard! That makes him more of a mystery than he already is, and explains his thinking about sidesaddles. She felt herself grow pale at the ramifications of his disclosure. He had been raised in a home of proper manners and would recognize even a minute slip. And she had acted casually about proprieties, feeling that no one in Idaho would know the difference. What a mistake that was! At least, her instincts about his mother had been right. She most definitely hadn't let the frontier contaminate propriety, and Alexa knew she would expect to be received with all due respect on Tuesday. She had waited until she was sure she would be.

"How long have you lived out here?"

"Ten years full time. Summers before that."

"Summers?"

"Mother had always wanted to visit the west, so when I was eleven she arranged a tour. We came by Pullman to San Francisco with many stops along the

107

way. Then we took the train up the coast to Seattle. Through mutual friends, Mother met Robert Hornbeck, banker and gentleman rancher. He persuaded her to return east along the northern route and pay a visit to a real cattle ranch . . . his. That brought us here. Robert Hornbeck and I got along so well, he asked if I could stay the rest of the summer. Robert wrote me regularly during the school year. In the spring when the rest of the boys went off to summer camps, I came to northern Idaho.''

"So the Rathrum Plain became your second home.''

"My only home. I lived for summers, the love of a good man, and the stability I found here. My natural father died the year before I graduated from college. Mother, after the proper mourning period, came west with me.

"Obviously she and Mr. Hornbeck fell in love and married.''

"Yes. I'd never seen Mother so happy.'' David stopped talking and stared at the floor.

Alexa wanted to ask why, but he seemed drawn into his own world and she felt her question would intrude. She waited quietly, hoping he wouldn't change the subject.

He looked at her, studied her with different eyes. She felt he scrutinized her in a way nobody ever had before. What was he expecting to find in her? She had no idea, so she steadily returned his gaze and waited.

Finally, he continued. "My father was a man obsessed with power and position. He was a self-made shipping magnate, and although he possessed great wealth, he had no social background. That made him unacceptable in Boston society. My mother was young, beautiful, with all the right relatives, but financially strapped. Mother never has said, but I concluded early on that it was a marriage of convenience. His money for her social connections. I always thought I was the result of the only union they ever had." He gulped and cast a shocked look at Alexa. "My apologies. You must be horrified," he gasped. "I got lost in my story and it just slipped out." His face went red then white as he agonized over his social gaffe.

She laughed softly. "I'm an Illinois farm girl, not a Boston debutante. Aunt Cassy trained me in manners, but she couldn't do much about the farm environment, so I don't shock readily." She hoped her comments would restore his calm. She wanted to hear the rest of the story. She was sure she would never hear this version from his mother.

"My father thought with Mother's connections, he would be accepted into Boston society, and he was. They were received at all the right places. He built a huge mansion and entertained all the right people in return. They spent summers in Cape Cod, autumns on the coast of France, and were in Boston for 'the season.' I spent those years in boarding schools." A bitter note crept into his voice.

The lonely little rich boy, Alexa thought. *How sad.* "It's hard for me to conceive your choosing to live here, and burying all your college training. It's almost as if those years were wasted."

"I use my business background at the bank. I enjoyed the life here tremendously until Dad Hornbeck died. I belonged to a family for the first time in my memory. Robert Hornbeck treated me like a son. I legally took his name because I loved him so much. I don't know who has suffered most over his death, Mother or me."

"Was his death sudden?"

"A heart attack at the bank. He was gone before Mother and I could even get to his side. That was two years ago. I'm only beginning to feel normal again and able to think about doing something with my life. My biggest concern is Mother. She entertains exquisitely,

109

has a whole host of good works she's active with, and manages an impeccably smooth house. However, she has never had any head for business nor any desire to learn. She loved it here in the west, but I can't leave her to run the ranch.'' His shoulders dropped forward into a slump of despair.

"Isn't there someone you could trust to manage the ranch business?''

"No one now. Mother and your Uncle Clyde got along famously. I don't know if marriage had been discussed, but he had her design and oversee the building of this house down to the towels in the bath, and stocking the kitchen with the proper utensils. It was a splendid diversion for her after Dad died. The house was finished just a few weeks before Clyde died. In fact, it was the day before the big open house Mother had been planning for weeks.''

"Your mother must be a very strong woman to survive such shattering blows and still go on so vigorously.''

"Boston breeding, my dear. One does not show one's emotions in public no matter how badly one hurts inside. And she is hurting for I know she greatly misses Clyde and is terribly concerned with what to do about our ranch.''

"Are you willing to stay and run it?''

There was an abnormally long pause and Alexa couldn't imagine why. Was he actually making up his mind about what to do? Perhaps he didn't want to give her a direct answer and didn't know how to tactfully skirt the issue. On second thought, that wasn't likely. Not with the training he had had. He would never be at a loss for the proper phrase or way to express himself.

"I'm not sure. I need a change. There isn't enough challenge to our ranch. I'd like to obtain more ground and do some experimenting with breeding. Doc Ward, our valley horse doctor, is very interested in trying his hand. I've taken some home study courses in veterinary medicine and I find it fascinating."

"That sounds like a most exciting thing to do. Why do you hesitate?"

"Our land doesn't grow adequate feed and our water supply is erratic. Not an ideal situation under which to pursue experiments in animal husbandry."

"Under those conditions, I can understand your reluctance to begin such an ambitious project." Alexa remembered his remarks earlier about her desirable land and water and now she realized what was bothering her. Were his attentions directed at her because he liked her or because he wanted her ranch? She didn't want to think it was the latter, but having had little in her life, she understood and recognized avarice when she saw it. It was time to change the subject. If it was the ranch he wanted and not her, she wasn't up to facing that fact right now.

Suddenly he moved from her and slid to the edge of the couch. Reaching for the book of poems she had been reading earlier, he read the title, then opened the cover and leafed the pages. "I've always envied Elizabeth and Robert Browning—their love and their ability to express it in immortal fashion."

"I, too, find that their poetry expresses the deep feelings of my heart as I shall never be able to. Which of hers is your favorite?"

"While I do find Sonnet 43 most moving, I have never loved with such depth and find it difficult to fully comprehend. Sonnet 26 captures both my experiences and dreams."

"Would you read it?" Alexa asked, remembering her earlier vision of his reading poetry to her. She hadn't dared hope it might be from Elizabeth Barrett Browning's *Sonnets from the Portugese* even though she had made the collection easily accessible.

He cleared his throat and moved to sit so he might see her well as he read.

"I lived with visions for my company
Instead of men and women, years ago,
And found them gentle mates, nor thought to know
A sweeter music than they played to me.
But soon their trailing purple was not free
Of this world's dust, their lures did silent grow,
And I myself grew faint and blind below
Their vanished eyes. Then Thou didst come to be,
Their songs, their splendors (better, yet the same,
As river water hallowed into fonts),
Met in thee, and from out thee overcame
My soul with satisfaction of all wants:
Because God's gifts put man's best dreams to
shame."

He raised his eyes to her and she saw in them a
forlorn, rejected young man sitting alone, trying to
find solace and understanding for his condition.

"You must have been terribly unhappy being left
alone so much," she said softly.

"I didn't know how miserable I was then. Most of
the boys in the dormitory were in exactly the same
situation so it seemed natural. Only after Mother and I
moved here did I realize how pitifully devoid of love
my earlier years had been. Mother feels terribly guilty
over her neglect, but her husband demanded that she
be with him and I can only imagine the tactics he used
to assure that his wishes were fulfilled."

"Hasn't your mother ever confided in you?"

"She never talks about him or their life together.
When she refers to that time, it's always about a
place, an event, or other people. I doubt I shall ever
know what she went through." He gently shut the
book and laid it back on the table. "Perhaps it's just
as well, since I can do nothing to change those years
for her or myself. The less known or remembered
about them the better."

All he was telling her came as a great shock to

Alexa. She had somehow thought if one were rich, life held no problems that couldn't be easily resolved. She thought one resided in a perfectly happy and carefree world. And here was David revealing to her that his childhood was even more barren than Martin's. The two men's revelations caused her to see that she herself had been reared in near-ideal circumstances.

He reached for her hand again. "Dear Alexa, you've been such a patient listener as I've burdened you with my unhappy past. I do wish to apologize. That was not my intent when I asked to call this evening."

"Unless people are willing to share the good and the bad, there can never be an honest relationship. I feel you have not shared these feelings with many people. Thank you for trusting me with them."

"You're very easy to talk with. You have a special quality of nurturing that makes one being in your presence feel safe and secure. Your Uncle Clyde had that same quality. I spent a great deal of time with him. He, more than any other, helped me reconcile my bitterness and accept my past as part of my present. Now, I have to learn to take what he taught me and move into my future."

"Have you tried prayer? I find I can talk with the Lord and I know exactly what I'm to do."

"I'm working on it. God has only come into my life in the last few years, and I still forget to turn to him on occasion."

There was a humility about David she hadn't sensed before. He really was trying to find his way. Silently, she vowed to pray diligently for him.

The chiming clock cut through the silence enfolding them. She felt him start at the sound. "I didn't realize it had grown so late. Here it is, ten o'clock and I haven't stopped talking about myself long enough to learn anything about you."

"How fortunate. Now you have an excuse to call again," she said, smiling.

"I don't need an excuse. I find I think about you most of the time, and finally the longing to see you grows until I can contain it no longer. I have to take the cattle out to the range and shall be away until Monday afternoon. I knew I had to see you before I left."

"I'm glad you did."

He slid his arm around her shoulders, and pulled her gently toward him. "I've waited a very long time for you to come into my life, but perhaps I wasn't ready until now to recognize an angel when God sent one to me."

Alexa could only blush at such extravagant praise. But she thoroughly enjoyed hearing it. Tilting her chin so their eyes met, he bent his head and kissed her. This time it wasn't the gentle, parting kiss she had expected. There simmered in his taking of her lips the deep longing of a man for a woman, the promise of an ecstasy she could only imagine. She slid her arms around his neck as he embraced her, drawing them together so closely so could feel the beating of his heart even through her shirtwaist. She withdrew her lips reluctantly and felt the throbbing of his heart in his throat. She felt his rapid pulse, strong with his desire for her.

She began to like all this too much. She felt control of her emotions slipping away. Moving back from him, she cradled the side of his face in her hand. "I fear for your safety if you tarry with me longer. The moon will soon be down and you will have no light with which to see."

"I know. I must go and yet I can hardly bring myself to leave you, knowing it will be Tuesday before I can see you again."

This time, however, she turned her cheek so that his kiss fell there. She had only herself to rely on for control and she wasn't sure how much will-power she would have if he kissed her a second time as passionately.

He accepted the rebuff, picked up his hat, and placing his arm around her shoulders, they made their way to the door.

"Goodnight, David. Have a safe trip to the mountains and I shall pray for you."

"Knowing you are thinking about me will keep me safe until Tuesday. But it won't do a thing to ease the longing for you," he said and took her hand. Again he left her with the imprint of his kiss tingling in her palm and on the inside of her wrist. Then, quite unexpectedly, he bent and claimed her mouth once more . . . gently, tenderly, lovingly. This kiss left her more helpless than the one earlier.

He placed his hat securely on his head and bounded down the steps and onto his horse. She stood watching as he rode away, the sound of the hoofbeats distinct in the still night air. She stood listening and watching until he became a misty shadow and the hoofbeats dulled to tiny muffled drums.

She put out the lamps and undressed in the dark. The beams of moonlight through the window gave her sufficient light to make her way to bed. Her mind was full of David and all that he had told her and she was a long time going to sleep.

Finally, as she began to doze off, she heard the kitchen door open and close. Alexa recognized Emmie's step. The step creaked as she crept up the stairs. Alexa remembered hearing the clock strike eleven. What on earth was Emmie doing outside at this hour?

CHAPTER 10

As ALEXA WALKED DOWN THE HALL TO BREAKFAST , she could hear Emmie humming contentedly in the kitchen. No telling how long the housekeeper had been up, but she usually never slept past five-thirty. That meant she'd had about five hours of sleep. Yet, as Alexa stood watching unnoticed in the kitchen doorway she observed that Emmie had never looked better. Freshly washed and curled up on her head in an imitation of Alexa's style, Emmie's normally mousy brown hair shone a soft fawn color, and her new calico dress rustled with starch as she moved briskly between sink and stove.

She set a pot full of water on the stove and turned to survey Alexa. "See you finally decided to start the day," she said in a flinty voice, but her face made a lie of her stern reprimand. The tired sag that caused her face to look older than her years was gone, and her eyes sparkled with a light not previously there.

There's only one thing brings out all this in a woman, Alexa thought. *A man.* She wondered if Emmie and Bill were attracted to each other. *But what about Emmie's husband, Luke?* Calloused as it seemed, if things were as bad as Emmie had indicated she would be a widow before long.

"You're mighty quiet this morning," Emmie commented when Alexa failed to respond. "Didn't things go well with Mister David?"

"Oh, yes, Emmie," Alexa assured her. She sat at the work table and watched Emmie dish up a bowl of hot cereal. "Things went just fine. He's going to take their cattle to summer range and will be gone until Monday," she said, making it sound as though he planned to be away several months.

"Poor boy, could not he leave you for three days without showin' up here?"

Alexa giggled. Put that way, it seemed quite ridiculous. "Apparently not," was all Alexa chose to say. Emmie wasn't going to bait her into revealing anything about last night. Knowledge of David's life was too new, and Alexa wanted time to savor the details and the emotions they aroused in her. She needed to sort those things meant for her only, from those she could share.

Alexa reached for the cream pitcher. "It's certainly a treat to have fresh cream for one's cereal," she said, changing the subject. "Is Jake content having the extra duty of milking the cow?"

Emmie sniffed. "I reckon. Calls her 'Pansy'. Brushes her and talks to her like a lover. I think he's workin' with half a deck, but Bill says it's good for the old man to have things to care for."

It delighted Alexa to have Emmie growing so crusty and independent. Little remained of the unkempt defeated soul who'd crawled out of the attic wardrobe. In fact, Emmie would be almost pretty were it not for that missing front tooth. Perhaps there was a dentist in Spokane experienced with false teeth. She must ask Jane Hornbeck on Tuesday.

Alexa looked up to see Emmie, arms akimbo,

standing in the middle of the kitchen floor staring at her. "You sure you're all right?" Emmie's voice had a definite edge of concern.

"I truly am. Why do you ask?"

"'Cause you keep driftin' off somewhere's while we're talkin'. Rather, I'm talkin', but you ain't listenin' or talkin' worth nothin'."

"I am listening. I've heard everything you've said.

"Then you're havin' trouble digestin' my talk 'cause there be some unnaturally long pauses between answers."

Alexa puzzled a minute over Emmie's accusation, then laughed. "Emmie Dugan, I am not going to tell you what went on last night between David and me. Rest assured, however, nothing unseemly occurred. He and his mother will be here Tuesday afternoon to pay a formal call, and I will receive them most properly and in good conscience."

"Hummph," Emmie snorted. "It still ain't proper to entertain a suitor without a chaperone. Temptation's gonna overtake you, girl. You mark my words." Thunder clouds of disapproval hung over Emmie's face and rolled through her voice.

Alexa sighed. *Shades of Aunt Cassy. Why was love so hard to live with sometimes?* "Emmie, I promise not to entertain suitors again in the house without a chaperone — though I didn't realize until late last night that the house was empty."

Emmie's face remained passive and she ignored Alexa's sharp reminder. "I should think so," she replied brusquely, but the softening of her features let Alexa know that Emmie was relieved at having extracted the promise. "Now, it's time you were off on your horse."

Alexa carried her bowl and glass to the sink and added them to the dishpan. "I do need to spend some time on the books, but I'm still stiff and sore, though nothing compared to yesterday."

"All your sufferin' be a waste if you don't finish workin' out the cramps. Turn right back to yesterday's worst, the next time you ride. Want that again?"

"Never! I'm going, I'm going. Don't wait any meals for me. I have no idea when I'll be back."

"Any idea where you're goin'?"

"I may go east today. Yesterday, I covered a lot of the land to the north and some on the west. I'd like to see the problem with the fences between Mr. Taylor's land and mine."

You're ridin' skirt's fresh ironed on the back of a chair in the sitting room."

Surprise flooded through Alexa at Emmie's grudging acceptance of the unapproved riding style, and she threw her arms about Emmie to bestow an extravagant hug. "I do appreciate you, Emmie, and all you do for me. Thanks."

Emmie kept her head tucked, but blushed her pleasure. "Get on with you, girl. If you insist on that heathen skirt, can't have it lookin' like a cat's bed."

Alexa hurried and changed. When she reached the barn, she could see Jake in one of the corrals. She walked to where he was piling more wood on a hot fire. Metal handles protruded from the fire, and Alexa recognized branding irons.

"How's the branding going?" she asked.

"A trifle slow. One of the new hands had a powerful thirst he tried to quench in one sittin'. Bill had to fire him so we're working one man short. We'll be fine, though. Goin' riding?"

"Yes, Emmie says I must or I'll never get over being sore." Alexa looked out into the pasture and sighed. "I love riding, but I do dislike having to walk a mile each time to get to Red."

"Whistle for him."

"I can't whistle. I've always been told it's unladylike."

119

"I guess it is, but sure saves steps when you need a horse in a hurry."

The idea intrigued her. "Can you teach me?"

"I can try. Whistle has to be loud or the horse won't hear."

"How loud?"

Jake demonstrated. It was shrill and piercing and Alexa clapped her hands over her ears. She watched as the horses raised their heads, and Red looked toward Alexa and Jake. Then Jake whistled again, and Red wheeled and trotted toward the barn.

"Oh, Jake, I am impressed. Is Red the only horse trained to come when you whistle?"

"Only one trained to that whistle."

Red arrived, blowing and snorting, and began nuzzling Jake. "Excuse me, Miss Alexa, gotta get some oats. Red expects a treat for obeyin'."

Alexa watched as Red followed Jake to the outbuilding where the oats were stored. While they were gone, she looked at her two little fingers. Some of Aunt Cassy's boys could whistle the way Jake just had, but they used the thumb and first finger on one hand. When she was about eleven, she'd practiced secretly for hours in an attempt to make that wonderful piercing sound, but the skill had eluded her.

Jake had whistled by placing the tip of the little finger of each hand in his mouth. Putting her fingers in her mouth the way she thought Jake did and blowing out the quick hard breath she'd seen Jake use, she produced a fine wind sound. She adjusted her tongue and tried again. Nothing. She was having no more success than when she'd tried years earlier. There was a definite purpose in learning now, though, and she vowed that with Jake's instruction, this time she would master it.

Jake returned with Red trailing him. He watched her futile attempts for a few minutes, then passed on by, leaving her to practice while he saddled Red for her.

When Jake returned, Alexa looked at him and sighed. "I think I'm missing some of the fine points of whistling."

Jake hobbled his way over to stand next to her. "Let me see how you're a doin' it?" He peered carefully at her as she demonstrated. "You ain't lickin' the tips afore you stick 'em in your mouth." He gave his fingers a quick swipe with his tongue before placing them in his mouth. "Now, curl your tongue up and put your fingers on top to hold it curled."

She did as he'd instructed, but nearly choked when she looked to see him bent over squinting intently into her mouth.

"Dad gum! That's the way. Now blow."

Alexa did, but her whistle sounded like wind whistling down the chimney. She looked at him and sighed again.

"Now, don't you go gettin' discouraged. You got the fundamentals right. Takes a lotta practice. You just keep at it and one day you'll surprise yourself and old Red, too."

"I'll keep working on it. Thanks for saddling Red for me."

Alexa swung into the saddle and rode out along the trail to the east. She quickly left the meadow and entered a stand of lodge pole pine reaching high over her head. She knew nothing about judging distances so couldn't even guess at their height. She must ask Martin when she saw him again. Alders, willows, mountain maple, and choke cherries provided dense cover and food for the abundant game Martin said lived in the forest. She rode into a small meadow with a creek flowing through.

As she neared a gurgling stream, she could smell the perfumed fragrances from the blooming plants along its banks. She dismounted and stood at the edge of one of the side pools. The scene reminded her of the Twenty-third psalm as she sat near the still water mirroring the sky and deep green shrubs. Looking down along the creek, she thrilled at stately cottonwoods forming a canopy of cathedral-like arches over the ever widening stream.

The sounds along the stream were far from church-like, though. The air was filled with the strident chatter of darting flickers and the clear sustained warble of handsome goldfinches. Ducks, the white bars of their wings beating out a primitive rhythm, sped above the sparkling water and lifted into the sky, quacking their delight. Alexa heard small, red-shafted birds she couldn't name add their drum-like tattoo to the cacophony as they hollowed out homes in the cottonwoods. She did recognize swallows as they emerged from their mud nests along the underside of the bank to swoop and dive for their breakfast of insects, plentiful in shrubs and trees.

Reluctant to leave the absorbing scene, she nevertheless had set out to make herself familiar with the east fence. She again mounted Red and turned him back along the trail.

Alexa rode through small groups of trees and then into lush meadows. A small trickle of water ran through every one. Was this what David had been referring to? Even she could see this was great cattle country.

This time when she rode into the trees, they didn't break into a meadow but became more and more dense, larger in diameter. Before she had ridden very long, she and Red were brought up short by a gated fence. *So this is the boundary.* She slid off Red and tied him to the branches of a fallen log. As she walked along the fence, she soon saw what Bill had been saying about loggers and fence repair. All along the boundary, the broken fence posts had been propped up with tree limbs. It didn't bespeak excellence, most definitely. But why were the fences in such condition?

She examined the broken posts. The wood wasn't rotted. What had caused the posts to snap like matchsticks? She must ask Martin about this. If this was normal each spring, then she needed a different type of fencing.

Returning to where Red nipped at the tops of tender grasses and low shrubs, she decided to ride on through the gate. This had to be Martin's property she entered, and he wouldn't mind her exploring a bit.

Deeper into the woods, the type of trees changed. Now they grew so tall that nothing but their deep green tips met in communion with the sun. They permitted only gauzy remnants of day to seep through to the forest floor below. Alexa rejoiced as occasional silver-white threads of sunlight escaped the barrier of thick branches to tack golden buttons of light to the forest floor. The dank, musty smell of eternally damp rotting vegetation lay heavy, and she felt an enchantment grow slowly inside her as she rode deeper into the muted silence. A silence, nourished through lack of expression, grew until it evolved into a living force. Even the thud of the horse's hooves became deadened, the life of their sound absorbed to feed the force.

Suddenly, Red's ears pricked forward and then she heard the sound, too. The distant screech and whine of a saw violated the spell and directed her to the right at a fork in the trail. She hadn't considered until this moment that she might not be welcome. However, having come this far and never having seen a lumber camp, curiosity drove her on.

She rode to the edge of the clearing and reined Red to a stop. Across the clearing, steam and smoke rose from the shed of the small sawmill backed up against a steep slope. The strident squeal of the saw echoed eerie and harsh against the denuded mountain covered with stumps, proof of the logging already completed. A short distance away stood the camp buildings built of roughhewn lumber—a cookhouse, bunkhouse, a rude shelter for the horses and oxen, a pigsty and chicken coop, a smokehouse, a cabin separate from the rest, and a few outhouses. The enormous surrounding forest contrasted to make the buildings seem as toys set out for play. Alexa felt herself begin to shrink and her comprehensions grow unclear in this Gulliver-type world. She wondered how the men who worked here kept their perspective.

Timidly, she urged Red forward, praying all the while that Martin was somewhere close and might see her. She would feel terribly foolish asking for him. At the thought, she started to turn Red about and leave before anyone noticed her. In the lull of the saw, however, she heard a voice call her name. She watched men's heads swivel in her direction as Martin came bounding out of the sawmill toward her.

He took out his handkerchief and wiped his hands and face as he approached. She saw his shirt, sweat-stained, with traces of sawdust still clinging to his shoulders. Gone was the Stetson and, in its place, a wide-brimmed hat well sprinkled with sawdust. He took it off and slapped it against his leg as he walked, dislodging the wood chips.

"Alexa, good to see you. I honestly didn't think you'd come for dinner, but I'm happy I was wrong." He reached up, clasped his hands around her waist and swung her to the ground.

"I didn't start out with that notion. I wanted to see the fence between our spreads for myself. Now that I have, I must say I'm not much impressed with your fence repair. A child could knock over those posts propping up the fence."

"Ah, but there's a large difference. A child is smart enough to know that. The cattle aren't."

"I examined the posts and there seems to be nothing wrong with them. Why are great distances of sound poles snapped off?"

"Snow lays on the fence and the weight breaks them."

Alexa considered his information. "Then it would seem we need a different type of fence. Isn't there something that could withstand the deep snow?"

"A notched log one would."

"Then why hasn't one been built. Uncle Clyde certainly had the money."

"Money wasn't his problem. It's mine," Martin admitted reluctantly. "Any idea how much fencing you're talking about?"

"Probably not," she was forced to concede.

"Miles."

"Oh," she said, and dropped the conversation as they grew close to a group of men. One stepped out and walked toward her, his body corded with sinewy muscles from years of hard labor, the lines of his face deep-creased from the elements.

"Flint's our camp boss," Martin said, introducing the two. "Miss Spence is Clyde's niece. Been out surveying her place and got a bit off the track."

"How do." He looked both embarrassed and pleased. "Mighty happy to have you in camp, ma'am. Mighty happy." And to prove his point, a big grin locked his mouth open.

Martin's curt nod sent the man back to his duties. Then Martin led her to the cookshack. "Better let Slim know there'll be a guest for dinner," he said. He pushed open the door and ushered her inside.

Alexa didn't know what she expected to find, but it wasn't this. The aroma of cake filled the room and she could hear meat sizzling on the big stoves. Two long tales stood spread with red and white striped oil cloth, while a tin plate and cup turned upside down marked each place. Wondering what one ate with, she lifted a plate and there lay the utensils covered against the ever-present flies. Unpainted backless benches lined the tables. Two men and a young boy were busy in the

125

kitchen part of the room. Martin introduced the three but took special pains to let her know the importance of Slim, the head cook.

Slim weighed three hundred pounds if he weighed an ounce, and Alexa had a hard time accepting a name that seemed to poke fun at a person's weakness or disability. She would have liked to know his real name, but now wasn't the time to delve into it. "I do hope I'm not an inconvenience," she apologized.

"Ma'am, you're as welcome as sunshine and clear weather anytime you want to drop by. Gets lonesome out here with nothing to look at but them bearded, ugly-faced loggers. Can't take time off to get to town when cutting weather's good. And when the weather's bad, it's so rotten even us desperate ones don't make the trek often." He turned to Martin. "You and the lady want to eat in your cabin."

"I think that might be best," Martin agreed. "I'll take her out to where they're cutting, let her see a big one go down. Be back in about an hour." He took her arm and guided her outside.

They hiked to an area where the men were working. Alexa watched, learning the rhythm of the crew as the big-muscled men moved in choreographed precision, each man knowing his job, yet each dependent on the other.

"Those are the fallers," Martin explained as he pointed to two men working together, cutting notches up a tree, then shoving springboards in to make a place to stand, removing them, and repeating the process until they were about fifteen feet above the ground. "They're getting up the tree away from the swollen pitch-filled base of the Douglas fir. The tree's about eight feet in diameter where they're going to start cutting. Watch, they're ready now for the first cut."

Alexa watched in awe as the two men swung their long, narrow double-bladed axes in synchronized

126

rhythm, one on each side of the emerging cut, one swinging right-handed, one left. It seemed impossible that two toy-sized figures chopping away at the mammoth tree could bring it down.

"The tree is about two-hundred-twenty-five feet tall." Martin's voice held a tinge of reverence.

The open wedge on the side of the tree grew ever wider as the fallers worked with their steady rhythm. They stopped and poured something from a can over their axes.

"They're pouring oil on their axes to thin the pitch that builds up," Martin told her. "Most of the crew use old whiskey bottles to do the job. Reminds them of the pleasure they had emptying them when they were new."

"I'd heard loggers were hard drinkers."

Martin chuckled. "Ma'am, you ain't heard the half of it." He pointed to the ground crew working beneath the tree. "These men aren't as showy as the fallers, but without them, we'd never get these monsters out of here. The swampers clear the under-bush so we can get to the other trees, the hooktenders determine the 'ride' or natural resting position of each log. They 'snipe' or chop the front end of the resting log round and smooth so it won't catch on the skidroad going down the mountain."

"Did I see the skidroad?" Alexa asked, trying to recall what he was talking about.

"No. It's made of skids—foot-thick timbers at least twelve feet long, laid like railroad ties and half buried in the ground." They walked over to a wide path through the trees and Martin explained what she was seeing. "The skids are spaced at seven-and-a-half-foot intervals so that the logs, all longer then sixteen feet, will always rest across two of them. A scallop is cut out of the top surface of each skid to cradle the passing logs."

"What are those men doing?" she asked, pointing

127

to men working alone, each around his own fallen tree.

"Those are the buckers. They cut the fallen trees into manageable lengths for the hooktenders who drive metal spikes into the logs. Next, they fasten chains which run forward through these—metal 'dogs' to the lead log and are hooked to the yokes of the oxen."

A large, burly man wearing a floppy hat, galluses over a bright red and black plaid shirt, and heavy caulked boots waved at Martin and then proceeded to bellow, "Hump, you, Buck! Move!" Then he cracked a whip in the air and Alexa watched eight pairs of huge oxen strain to move the string of about a dozen chained-together logs, each about five feet thick.

"Each log weighs about five tons," Martin said. "Those Durham oxen are some of my most valuable assets, and Bull babies them like they were family."

All the while Martin had been instructing her in the fine points of logging, Alexa couldn't keep her eyes from straying back to the aerial dance of the fallers. Martin followed her glance. "That tree won't come down today, but if you don't mind walking a bit farther into the woods, I can show you one that will."

"Oh, yes. I do want to see the final reward for all that effort and assure myself that it is possible for midgets to accomplish such a mighty task. Really makes one a believer in the David and Goliath story, doesn't it?"

"I hadn't thought of it, but you're right."

She felt him suddenly grab her arm. She had been gawking so at her surroundings, she had nearly tripped over a large tree root growing across the trail. "Thanks. Guess I'd better watch where I'm walking."

"It's hard to keep your eyes on the ground when there's so much beauty above your head."

At last they arrived where a giant fir was nearly

ready to go down. Martin pointed to a slender stake driven in the ground. "That's the guide mark for where the tree should fall."

Alexa watched as two fallers, using only their axes and one springboard each, made cuts in the base of the tree up as far as they could reach, thrust the board in, and hauled themselves up. Then, after making another cut high above their heads, they drove their axes deep into the trunk and stood on them while they pulled out the boards and wedged them into the higher cuts and swung up to them.

"That's incredible the way they're climbing up that tree," Alexa gasped.

Martin chuckled. "They're putting on a bit of a show for you. Word came up the hill you'd be here to watch the fall."

At last the two men were in position opposite the undercut, about twenty feet above the ground. "They'll make the backcut now. That takes away the last support from the tree." Even Martin spoke in hushed tones as a ritualistic silence settled over the men. As many times as they had seen this, Alexa felt the anticipation of those who watched. Each man eyed the tree and checked his position to be sure he was out of harm's way.

The only sound in the deep woods was the ringing of the fallers' axes. It was as though the forest and all who dwelt there united into one force hanging suspended, breathless, out of respect for the last moments of life of a giant, centuries old.

Time stopped, began again in slow motion, and Alexa felt drawn into the vortex of the unfolding drama. The cry, "Timber!" cut the measured silence just before the anguished groan of the tree, a cracked, whining roar, rent the air. Goliath crashed and the earth shuddered with the impact.

She saw and heard it all and would have screamed had not Martin seen it coming and clamped his hand over her mouth, damming up the release of the emotions aroused at the marauding band who dared desecrate God's handiwork. Alexa saw the fallers fling their axes through the air. She watched the axes slowly spin their way to the ground, watched the fallers leap and fall, endlessly in the time alteration.

Floating debris wavered through the air, through the moment of absolute silence, consecrating the spot. A final benediction beat upon the heart, demanding remembrance of this irreplaceable tree, growing here while Vikings walked the land on the east coast. The felled titan sighed its last settling noises, and the men broke into whoops of joy.

Martin took his hand away and Alexa didn't make a sound. She sagged against him, burying her face in his chest and trembling against him. She tried to say what filled her, but choking sobs came out instead.

He patted her back and held her head close to him with his other hand. "I'm sorry, Alexa. I couldn't let you scream. You'd have startled the men, and they might have missed their spot. For safety's sake, they throw their axes first and then jump clear just before the tree goes down. I should have warned you, though. I just didn't think. I've seen this so many times."

She pushed away from him and turned to see the two fallers receiving congratulations and jokes from the ground crew but looking anxiously her way. She managed a thin smile and a small wave. They seemed satisfied and each gave her a clumsy bow.

Her attention was again drawn to the fallen tree. She looked for the stake but saw the tree lay directly in the path, burying the stake. The fallers had been extremely accurate. She tipped her head back to see the gaping hole left in the green roof of the forest. Blue sky shown through and a shaft of sun found the opening and pierced the dimness, spotlighting the stump, the ugly remnant left as a testimony to the glory that had once stood there. The air still carried the turbulence and scent of upheaval, the scent of dust, decaying matter, the odor of death.

She had witnessed a murder, heard the groan of the victim, helpless under the tiny but deadly axes. She had seen the final death throes.

Alexa turned back to Martin, churning inside, knowing her mouth trembled with still unshed tears. A vision of death still raged inside her, the final swaying, the frozen instant of motionlessness, the falling . . . all etched indelibly onto her mind.

"I know the wood is needed for so many things and there are so many trees, but it's like watching a fragment of eternity die, never to be duplicated or replaced."

Martin took her face in his hands and looked deep into her eyes. "I know," he said, his voice a choked whisper. "I felt it the first time with agonizing clarity. I'm still not free of it."

She stared into the gun-metal gray of his eyes and marveled at the complexity of him. The man who could mourn the death of an ancient forest while engineering its extinction. She understood now the feeling in the valley against Martin and his men. The people who had seen these trees, felt their power, also mourned their deaths and helpless to punish their killers, hated them the more.

"How can you continue to destroy the forest?" Alexa asked.

Martin's face closed, his eyes turned opaque, and he shrugged. "It's a living." Abruptly he turned and left to talk with one of the men.

She stood alone. The feeling of desolation crept through her, leaving her cold and fraught with frustration.

CHAPTER 11

JANE HORNBECK AND DAVID CAME TO CALL on Tuesday. Alexa poured tea from the carefully polished tea service and Emmie served lemon tarts with whipped cream. Everyone was very proper and mannerly, and Alexa, instead of enjoying the afternoon she had looked forward to for so long, found it boring. Jane Hornbeck couldn't help letting her longing to be mistress of the beautiful house show and Alexa felt sorry for her. It would be hard to build and furnish your dream house and then watch someone else inherit it.

David hovered over his mother like a moth around a flame, anticipating her every wish. His attentions seemed overdone and left Alexa wondering why he found such solicitude necessary. The Hornbecks stayed the required time and then left promptly with the promise to come by at seven-thirty on Saturday evening to take her to the social.

"It's Thursday, Miss Alexa. Don't you think it's time to start thinking about decorating your box?" Emmie reminded her.

"Yes. What size box do you want, Emmie? Long as I'm getting mine, might as well find one for you, too."

"Don't believe I'll be going." Then something else occurred to her. "Are Bill and Jake planning to attend?"

"I think Jake is, but I can't say about Bill." Emmie left abruptly for the garden without further discussion.

When Alexa heard Emmie return from harvesting the garden, she came into the kitchen and asked, "Emmie, do you have any idea where I might find some paint?"

"Attic's only place I can suggest." Emmie set a kettle on the stove and gave her full attention to Alexa. "What you doing with two boxes?" Suspicion brought back the wariness to her eyes.

"Fixing you a box. You have to go, Emmie, and so do Jake and Bill. I'll not have it said I wouldn't give the Bar S Ranch help time off for the box social."

"Heard this was a free country," Emmie said, sullen and uncooperative. "Thought we could do as we wanted."

"Not when it looks bad for the ranch, you can't. This social is to raise money. You're not going to make it look like I don't pay you enough to furnish a proper box, or I'm such a slave driver you can't get time away to go to the party. Either way, a lie is born. If you don't want to stay for the dancing, that's fine, but you all *have* to go to the social."

"I'm no good with this sort of thing," Emmie said. "If you insist I have a box, you're gonna have to do the decorating."

"I love decorating boxes. I won't mind doing yours. When was the last time you went to a social?" Alexa asked.

"Never have been," Emmie said in a low voice.

"You've never been to a box social!" This confession was nearly impossible for Alexa to comprehend. "Never, in your whole life? What have you done for fun?"

"Never had time for fun. As young'uns, we lived too far in the hills to come out for such nonsense. Didn't have no money for doodads to decorate a box with or fancy food to put in it."

"A couple times after I got big and left home. I ain't real good, though. Got two left feet." Emmie acted nervous as talk of the dance proceeded, twisting her hands in her apron and shifting her weight from one foot to the other. Then her face brightened. "I ain't got a proper dress to wear. Wouldn't do me being seen without corsets and a decent dress."

Alexa looked up at her. "Emmie Dugan, you're not going to get out of going on such flimsy grounds. I'll take you to town for corsets, and I have plenty of time to make you a dress or a skirt and shirtwaist, whichever you'd feel more comfortable wearing. Emmie, you are going to that social, like it or not. It'll be a lot more fun if you decided to like it."

Deep worry lines altered Emmie's face and she looked absolutely miserable. "Don't guess you're giving me much choice."

"Do you want a shirtwaist and skirt, or a dress?" Alexa asked. We may have fabric here that would do."

"I'm thinking the skirt outfit would be more serviceable."

"So do I."

By the time they were ready to leave for town, the worry lines in Emmie's face had subsided, to be replaced by a happy glow. After they were seated in the buggy and clattering down the road, Emmie confided to Alexa, "I ain't never had a new corset. Not in my whole life. Always had a good enough figure for my work and when I needed to, I had a second-hand one I'd get on."

Emmie's confession touched Alexa although it was hard for her to conceive of any woman reaching maturity without having several corsets for different occasions. "What kind of work were you in?" Alexa asked innocently.

When Emmie didn't answer, Alexa turned to see an angry blush creep up Emmie's neck and she looked extremely uncomfortable. "Only kind I knew to do, with no education and living in roaring mining towns. Actually, that's how I met Luke. Found we both wanted to change our ways so we lit out together. Stopped in Cheyenne on our way up here and tied the knot. We was honeymooning when he got dragged off to jail."

Alexa reached over and placed her hand over Emmie's ungloved knotted fingers moving nervously in her lap. "I didn't mean to pry, but I thank you for sharing something of your past with me. The Lord will forgive you your sins if you have a sincere heart. All you have to do is ask."

Emmie sat with bowed head. She didn't speak again until they neared town. "I'd like to believe what you've told me is true."

"It is, Emmie. All any of us has to do is repent of our sins, take the Lord Jesus Christ as our Savior, and try to sin no more."

"I'd sure like to get washed clean and get Luke to do the same."

"There must be an itinerant preacher who comes through here. I shall ask at the social. I don't know what you can do about Luke, though. I suppose they have a preacher for the prisoners. I can find out about that too, if you'd like."

Emmie smiled and nodded. Alexa beamed with joy. She hadn't expected this trip to yield such rich rewards.

They located a lady's apparel shop, small but elegantly stocked, and Emmie was fitted with a fine steel-ribbed, sateen-covered corset. It was remarkable how much better she looked even in the unstylish calico. "I declare, Emmie Dugan, you'll be the belle

of the social when we get you a proper outfit made,"
Alexa bubbled.

Emmie again reddened under the unaccustomed
praise. "Ain't no one gonna compete with you," she
said softly.

Alexa stopped at the large drygoods store and
purchased the few items she needed. The two women
arrived home early enough that Alexa had time to cut
out Emmie's skirt before supper.

"You won't get your ridin' in today," Emmie
observed as they finished the dishes.

"As soon as I hang up this dishtowel and have my
talk with Bill, I intend to take a short ride.

Bill, Jake, and the other two hands were lazing on
the log bench set against the bunkhouse when she
broke out of the trees and approached them. Bill
stood and walked to meet her. Together they strolled
toward the barn and discussed the ranching activities
as they went.

"There's one other thing I've failed to mention,"
Alexa said. "Saturday night, the school board's
holding a box social and square dance. Since the other
men don't belong permanently to the valley, I
wouldn't be upset if they stayed away, but I'd
appreciate it if you and Jake made plans to attend."

Bill took off his hat and scratched his head.
"Hhmmph," He cleared his throat. "I already give
the boys permission to go into town. They been
working real steady and have a need to blow off a
little steam. That leaves the place alone if I was to go,
too. Don't think that's wise. With everybody gone,
Indians'll take it as an invitation to help themselves. I
do believe it'd be good business to lock the house up
tight, but leave a fire banked so it shows smoke. I'll
stay and make my presence known both up here and
around the house."

Alexa stood gaping at him. "Indians! I haven't seen
a single one in all my travels."

"But they've seen you. Reservation's not far away. They have free access to your land. They ride across the place all the time, but don't you try the same privilege with theirs," Bill warned.

"Well, under the circumstances, I suppose it would be wise to leave someone here," she conceded.

"You can bet the rest of the ranches will," he said, returning his hat to his head and looking tremendously relieved.

Bill left her and sauntered back to join the crew. Alexa, dashing to the edge of the pasture, licked her thumb and first finger, placed them against her teeth, and blew. Martin had demonstrated this method when she had showed him Jake's style. This seemed more comfortable than the two little fingers and took only one hand. She practiced religiously each day, but she was still unable to produce more than a loud windy sound. She refused to give up, though. If Jake and Martin could do it, so could she.

Carefully, she moistened the fingers and reset her position. Arching her tongue just so, she blew again producing a fine blast. Red left his grazing and came trotting up to the barnyard. "That's a good horse," she crooned as she fed him oats.

Red soon stood saddled and ready. The muscles in her left leg had strengthened greatly. By grabbing the saddle horn and jumping a few times on her right foot, she could pull herself into the saddle.

Sitting firmly in the saddle, and pushing back solidly against the cantle, she fell into the rhythm of the horse and found herself riding with him instead of meeting him somewhere in the middle of his stride and slapping against the saddle seat. It was such times that kept her coming back again and again.

The light prevailing wind from the north began cooling the Plain and Alexa slipped into her cloak. She never tired of watching night come. It brought a peaceful hush over the busy sounds of the day. She stopped to watch some deer and a large elk feeding on the willows and other shrubs growing in the marsh. She sat, entranced by the does with their young, until she heard slow, soft hoofbeats coming toward her. Her heart leaped into her throat. Indians? And here she was, a good distance from home. Alone. Red felt her panic and he started to shake his head, prance sideways, and refuse to respond to the reins on his neck. She pulled the bit tight in his mouth and bowed his neck to keep him from bolting.

While she was thus occupied, a horseman rode into view. "What's the matter with Red?" Martin called.

Alexa breathed a sigh of relief. When Martin was closer, she said, "I thought you were Indians and Red reacted to my fear."

"Who's been scaring you about the Indians?"

"Bill said they could see me but I couldn't see them, and they rode over my ranch all the time."

"He's right about that, but there's no need to be afraid. They won't hurt you." King fell into step beside Red and they continued slowly down the road.

"What brings you out of the woods this evening?" Alexa asked.

"Exactly that. The woods. I start feeling real hemmed in some nights."

Alexa didn't know why she suddenly felt so elated. After all, he was nothing more than a friend and a casual one at that. "You planning to go to the social and dance Saturday night?" she asked.

"I hadn't given it much thought. Probably not, now that you call it to my attention."

"I think that's a mistake. It doesn't seem you're very well liked in the valley as it is. Might help people's opinion of you if you came and spent some money on a good cause."

"I don't think anything I might do would change public opinion of me or my men. As a whole our reputation is even more tarnished than the miners' and that's saying a lot."

"And I think you're wrong. If you were to present yourself looking like a gentleman, beard and hair trimmed, wearing a proper suit of clothes, you just might be surprised at your reception. You're quite handsome . . . or could be. The young things would no doubt swoon all over you."

"And what about you?"

"I'm a bit old for swooning, but I would save a dance for you." She lowered her head and batted her eyes extravagantly at him.

He chuckled. "With such bait coming from underneath that cowboy hat, how can I refuse?"

Martin escorted her back to the ranch and helped unsaddle Red. Somehow, Alexa didn't want Martin to ride away. "Won't you come down to the house for a piece of Emmie's blueberry pie?"

"You have more than one way to tempt a man, haven't you? You could become downright dangerous if something isn't done to control you."

"Any suggestions?" she teased back.

"Yes, but I'd prefer not having an audience while I demonstrate."

Looking over at the bunkhouse, she waved at the men still lounging against the side. She could feel their eyes on her as Martin led her along the path into the trees and out of their sight.

"There, that's better," he said, stopping in the trail and pulling her to him.

Startled, she looked up into his shadowed eyes, then realized his intent. A small shiver of anticipation ran through her. Their previous kisses had been those of compassion and caring. This time promised to be different. As he bent over her, she closed her eyes and raised her lips to meet his. They met gently at first, then she wound her arms about his neck and the kiss turned more intense. She felt a rush of liquid fire pouring through her veins and a low groan escaped from him as he attempted to draw her even tighter to him.

Little warning signals went off in her head and she knew she must put an end to this or they would both be lost. Slowly she removed her arms and placed her fingers on his cheeks. She drew herself away, breaking the kiss. Not willing to let her escape entirely, he enfolded her to him and held her tightly against his chest. She could feel the wild beating of his heart and knew it matched her own.

Now what was she going to do? She had thought no one but David could bring about such a response in her. And yet here she stood, content in the circle of Martin's embrace, moved emotionally by his kiss as she had been by no other. *Alexa, you're a wanton woman with no morals whatsoever. It would serve you right if neither man had any more to do with you.*

Preparations for the box social and square dance occupied every minute of the rest of the week. Coupled with her determination to ride every day, Alexa was left with little time for anything else. She refused to allow any thought of Martin to form, and speculation on how David would handle three passengers in the buggy with Mrs. Hornbeck as chaperone. She had the horrible feeling she would be expected to ride alone in the second seat while his mother sat in front beside him.

As Saturday grew closer, the vision of this awkward arrangement crossed her mind more often, but she managed to dispel it quickly.

CHAPTER 12

SATURDAY MORNING DAWNED in another cloudless sky. It hadn't rained a drop since Alexa arrived. Hadn't even seriously clouded up.

She rushed to the sewing machine to finish Emmie's skirt.

"Land child, you're sewing with a hot needle and galloping thread!" Emmie exclaimed as she stepped into the sewing alcove.

"I am, but I only have to stitch one more row of wide lace to trim the bottom and your skirt will be finished," Alexa answered. "How are you coming in the kitchen?"

"Jake's making the supreme sacrifice and parting with two of his prize roosters so we can have fried chicken. Said he would bring 'em down soon as he gets 'em plucked."

Alexa continued to pump the treadle vigorously while they visited.

"I ain't wearin' a corset. Wouldn't fit worth nothin'. I know it'll be just fine," she said.

Feet scraping on the back porch alerted Emmie that

Jake had arrived with the chickens. She hurried away, leaving Alexa to her final stitching.

After pressing the skirt, Alexa carried it upstairs and placed it on Emmie's bed next to the blouse and new undergarments Emmie had already laid out. *These are probably the nicest clothes she's ever had. She's trying not to show it, but I think she's really excited about tonight.* Alexa couldn't help singing as she tripped happily down the stairs.

Tying on an apron, Alexa presented herself in the kitchen. "What can I do to help?"

"You can stay out of the way," Emmie answered curtly.

Taken aback, Alexa crossed to the sink where Emmie scrubbed the chickens with much more vigor than they seemed to warrant. "Emmie?" Alexa peered into Emmie's face.

Emmie turned away, but not before Alexa saw the tears glistening on her cheeks. "Emmie, tell me this instant what's troubling you," Alexa demanded. But her words seemed to fall on deaf ears.

"Emmie! I must know why you're crying."

"You know, Miss Alexa. You're the cause." Emmie brushed Alexa aside and carried the pan full of chicken to the work table.

The accusation caught Alexa completely by surprise and left her dumbfounded. "Whatever are you saying? I wouldn't knowingly do anything to cause you grief."

Emmie faced Alexa, hands on her hips. "Jake says Bill's not going. Says he has to stay and look after things."

Righteous indignation poured through Alexa. How dare Bill make it sound as if she was forcing him to remain behind. "That was Bill's decision. I practically threatened to dismiss him if he didn't attend the social, but he insisted it was necessary to have someone here in case the Indians decided to annex us into their reservation."

Emmie looked at the floor. "That the truth?"

"It most certainly is. Ask Bill.

Alexa watched as the floured chicken pieces sizzled in the hot grease and slowly turned a tempting golden brown. Mulling the problem over in her mind, Alexa guessed Emmie had been counting on Bill to buy her box. She knew no one else she would feel comfortable with. And then Alexa smiled. There was one other person Emmie knew, and he promised he would be there "if nothin' broke or come untwisted". All Alexa had to do was make sure Jake knew which box was Emmie's. It solved another dilemma. She and Emmie would ride together in the back seat of the Hornbeck's buggy.

The rest of the day sped by and almost before Alexa knew it, it was time to bathe and dress.

While Alexa fixed her hair, she kept an ear tuned to the familiar creak of the third step from the bottom that would let her know when Emmie arrived in the downstairs hall. Much as Alexa enjoyed wearing her own finery, she could hardly wait to see Emmie in hers. The creaky signal came just as Alexa placed the last comb in her upswept curls. She dashed into the hall. There stood an unrecognizable Emmie.

Alexa couldn't contain a gasp of surprise. "Emmie! You look absolutely beautiful."

Emmie smiled without revealing any teeth and so kept the striking image intact. "Don't look too bad, do I?"

"Bad! You have a marvelous figure.

"'Course, having an exclusive dressmaker helps. Designs originals for me," Emmie said and sashayed down the hall to the kitchen.

Alexa's laughter pealed through the house. She was delighted that Emmie's good humor had returned. She had prayed all day for this. *Thank you, Lord, for hearing and answering my prayers.*

The wagon yard was full when they arrived, but David drove their buggy inside.

David assisted his mother from the buggy, as Alexa and Emmie quickly jumped out to help Jake place their supper boxes with the other baskets and boxes already assembled.

David drove the buggy away and Mrs. Hornbeck nodded pleasantly toward a group of women seated on benches under the trees. They were talking and fanning with equal speed, but everything halted as Jane Hornbeck, with Alexa in tow and Emmie following respectfully behind, sailed into their midst.

"Girls, I want you to meet Clyde's niece, Alexa, and her housekeeper, Emmie."

Names began dropping at a rapid rate and Alexa could not keep track.

"And this beautiful lady is our school teacher, Miss Helen Bearnson," Jane Hornbeck said, her manner growing formal and aloof despite the warm words.

Helen truly was beautiful. Tall, stately of bearing, soft blond hair and a winsome face. The fiber of strength in her character made itself felt even among the adults. She was a lady from the dotting of her 'i's' to the color of her ribbons. *Can't imagine a child ever trying to test her,* Alexa thought. And, Mrs. Hornbeck's accent on the word 'Miss' hadn't escaped her.

"I've heard how lovely you are," Helen said to Alexa. "The reports were not exaggerated. Welcome to our valley."

"Thank you. I've loved every minute so far." Alexa liked her immediately, but grew confused at the messages Jane Hornbeck sent. Did she or didn't she approve of the teacher? Or in his mother's eyes, was there no woman good enough for David Hornbeck? Had Alexa's coming interrupted a budding romance between David and Helen or was David considered the catch of the valley with every eligible girl setting her cap for him? Helen didn't look the type to chase a man. Alexa determined to watch the evening's proceedings very closely.

Her help was needed at one of the booths and Helen Bearson excused herself. Mrs. Hornbeck stopped to chat with friends, and Alexa and Emmie were at last free to wander about.

Wires were strung between the trees, and old sheets and blankets were pinned up to form small booths. Inside each odd shaped booth, a game, contest, or entertainment run by Helen's students enticed the citizenry to part with pennies or nickels. There was a ring-toss and pin-the-tail-on-the-donkey. A long line of little children stood in front of the fish pond. At the camera booth, the children allowed a father to operate the camera, but they took the money and posed the patrons.

"Want to knock over some pins with a baseball?" Alexa asked Emmie.

"Not me. Never could throw straight."

Alexa paid her nickel for three balls. Taking careful aim, she grasped the ball and let it fly. Pins sailed in all directions.

"Bet Aunt Cassy never caught you playing second base," Martin's voice said from behind her, a soft chuckle breaking up the sentence.

Without looking at him, Alexa laughed. She didn't tell him she had practiced pitching on the sly for years. "Can't be a lady all the time." She claimed her prize, a crocheted pot holder, then turned around. When she saw Martin, her mouth dropped open. Here stood a perfectly groomed gentleman in an expensive well-cut gray pinstripe suit. He hadn't forsaken the Stetson, but it was a soft gray to match the suit and his eyes. And he wore fine black leather boots, highly shined.

"I don't believe I've had the pleasure," she said softly.

Martin doffed his hat with a fine flourish. "David Hornbeck isn't the only dandy in the country."

Alexa ignored the remark. "I'm glad you decided to come."

"So am I. It was worth it to see you splatter those pins. And now would you introduce me to this lovely lady?" Martin turned his full attention to Emmie.

"May I present Mr. Martin Taylor . . . Mrs. Emmie Dugan."

"I'd never have recognized you, Emmie. You look like a picture from *Godey's.* "

"And how would you know that?" Alexa asked.

Now it was Martin's turn to laugh. "One of the boys in camp has a subscription. Keeps us right up to date on the latest in women's wear . . . from the skin out."

Unable to contain a full laugh, Emmie spread her fan across her mouth. But Alexa, having memorized each monthly issue for years, pictured Martin's inferences precisely and blushed uncontrollably. She could only think to retreat until she could collect herself. He might be dressed like a gentleman, but he sadly lacked refinement.

"Oh, Alexa," Helen Bearson called, her voice cutting through Alexa's churning thoughts. "I think Doc Ward's about to begin the auction. If you're free, would you mind helping serve coffee?"

"I'd be most happy to," Alexa answered, grateful for something to keep her busy.

"Doc Ward's our local veterinarian," Helen explained, not realizing Alexa knew. "He says he's going to run for the senate this fall, but I don't think he has much chance of being elected. If he wins, the folks in these parts will be without a horse doctor, and they'll never let that happen."

Alexa and Helen began setting the cups in their saucers and checking the sugar and creamers. "If he has no chance of winning, why is he going to run?" Alexa asked. He didn't sound awfully bright.

"He's been trying to get Jane Hornbeck to notice him since Robert passed on, but she's only had eyes for your uncle. Came as a terrible shock when he died so suddenly. I surmise Doc thinks if he does something terribly respectable and a bit exciting like getting elected to congress and can offer her Washington D.C., she might give him a tumble."

"I don't think Doc Ward has a chance as long as she has David to do her bidding. If David decided to leave the valley or take himself a wife, I suspect Mother would jump into the first open arms extended her way."

"Unfortunately, I doubt that David will consider marriage until he is sure Mother is well-taken of. Turns into a stand-off," Helen said, and a look of longing crossed her face as her eyes sought out David across the school yard.

During a lull in the bidding, Alexa turned to set out more cups and saucers. Several men passed slowly behind her visiting as they walked. She couldn't help overhearing their conversation. "Heard the facts right from the sheriff's deputy. Says the fellow got clean away on 'em as they was taking him from Coeur d'Alene to Boise City."

"I say we ought to do somethin'. Ain't safe having a murdering train robber running loose. Just might all wake up dead one morning. Kilt in our sleep, helpless as new babes."

"What kinda something you got in mind?"

"Well, I'm toting my gun. Leastways, I'll have some protection."

"Looking at the size o' that hunk a metal, what you'll have is a rupture."

The men all laughed and the subject changed. Apparently they weren't unduly concerned about Luke's escaping up into the valley. Alexa knew better, though. That explained Emmie's immediate and long disappearances each evening after supper. She knew where Luke was and obviously visited him as frequently as possible. She hadn't been upset that Bill couldn't come to the social. Emmie had planned to spend this evening with Luke, and Alexa had spoiled the plans by nearly forcing Emmie to come to the social. *Probably going to make up a fancy box and have Luke to the house for a private party.* Deep in thought, Alexa turned around in time to see Emmie's box go up for auction.

The oooh's and aaah's of appreciation caused Emmie to beam with pleasure. "What am I bid for this beautiful box?" Doc Ward boomed in his best senatorial voice.

Jake leaped to his feet. "Fifty cents!"

"Must be something special about this box for the gentleman to open the bid so high."

There is, Alexa thought. *His chickens.*

"Seventy-five cents," an unknown bidder countered.

"One dollar," Jake shouted at him.

"One twenty-five."

"One fifty."

Some people came for coffee and Alexa lost track of the bidding. By the time she could return to it, Jake's face had turned beet-red and he was mopping sweat with a large handkerchief. The silence thickened as Jake counted and re-counted his money. Then she saw a hand slip him a bill.

"Ten dollars and fifty cents!" Jake shouted triumphantly.

A number of over-sized people had formed a phalanx in front of Alexa and she couldn't see who was bidding against Jake.

"Ten seventy-five," came the muffled reply, so soft Alexa could scarcely hear it.

Jake stood defeated and more woe-begone than anyone she had seen in ages as Doc Ward intoned, "Going once, going twice, going three times. Gone! Pay the clerk, Mr. Taylor, and claim your girl."

Martin Taylor! Martin had bought Emmie's box! Alexa's hand shook as she poured the next few cups

148

of coffee. Things weren't turning out as she had planned at all.

"David, my boy," Doc Ward called. "Come, run this auction. I want to bid on the next basket coming down the aisle."

Alexa stopped pouring coffee and watched Jane Hornbeck's basket being set on the auction table. Doc Ward moved into the audience and opened the bidding. His rancher friends had a great time bidding against him even though they were all married. Their wives encouraged the bidding until Doc let it be known he was near the end of his bankroll.

"Sold to Doc Ward. Will the owner please claim her basket?" David pronounced, somehow managing to keep a straight face.

David jumped off the auctioneer's stump and went to stand with a group of rough-looking men. They must be single to look that unkempt, Alexa concluded.

"Oh, there goes mine," Helen whispered, and she strained forward.

The bidding for Helen's basket was vigorous and soon ran into the teens. There was much laughter and shouted comments, especially from the group around David, as the bidding climbed higher. Finally, when it appeared a particularly tough looking man from the group was going to buy Helen's box, David entered the bidding, and it took a turn from friendly to nearly open warfare. The man glared fiercely at David, then dropped to his knees and emptied his pockets spreading out all his bills and change on the ground. "Someone loan me some money. I'm good for it," he bellowed. Several of his companions responded and the bidding continued. Helen kept a passive face, but Alexa noticed she held the coffee pitcher with a white-knuckled hand.

When the men could raise no more money, David won the bidding and Helen's basket. Now it was

Alexa's turn to pour coffee with a clenched hand. Martin and David had made their purchases. Who would buy her box?

She was so deep into her misery she didn't realize it was her box up for bids until Jake again leaped to his feet. "Five dollars!"

Several men bid against Jake, but he was relentless and finally, Doc Ward pronounced him the winner for thirteen dollars and fifty-seven cents. Jake turned and gave Alexa a delighted smile before he shuffled down the aisle to pay the clerk and claim his prize.

He came to stand in front of her. "I came here promising my tonsils fried chicken and I dad-blamed ain't about to disappoint 'em."

"I can't think of anyone I'd rather eat with," Alexa said, hoping the Lord would forgive her the white lie.

"Looks like the folks is saving us a spot," Jake said and pointed to David and Helen who were motioning them over. Jake almost pranced as he carried Alexa's box toward the table where Martin and Emmie were already seated next to David and Helen. Doc Ward came to join the group proudly escorting Jane Hornbeck. Alexa fervently wished she was anywhere else, but there seemed no graceful way out. She sat as inconspicuously as possible at the far end of the table, making sure Jake sat next to Mrs. Hornbeck. David and Helen moved down and David, across the table from Alexa, gave her a gentle, wistful smile.

Helen looked at David with warm and grateful eyes. "Thank you for rescuing me,' she said as she dished up their supper.

"I wouldn't allow him to buy your basket. He had been drinking heavily, and I couldn't persuade him not to bid for it. Seems those fellows heard about our beautiful school marm and came up from Coeur d'Alene to pay you a call."

Alexa grew misty-eyed at David's gallantry. He hadn't rejected her, after all. And she was sitting across from him which was nearly as good as sitting next to him.

"David," Doc boomed. "I heard the state of Idaho is working on an exhibit for the World's Columbian Exposition to be held in Chicago next year. A friend told me they needed someone to be in charge of it. Right away, I thought of you. Said to bring you next time I came down to Boise City. I'm going next week. Interested?"

David glanced sideways at his mother. "W—W— why, yes," he stammered. "I'd like to hear what they're planning."

Mrs. Hornbeck looked aghast. "What are you saying, David? How can you think of leaving with all there is to do on our ranch? And what will Alexa do without you to help her?"

Doc answered for David. "Nothing needs doing right now, Jane, that won't wait 'til we're back. Boy needs to get out of here and down to the city. Been cooped up here for months without a break. We'll only be gone a week at most."

Martin, grinning like a cheshire cat, said, "And I'll be glad to look in frequently on Alexa during David's absence. Make sure everything's running smooth at the ranch. Check on your place too, if you like."

Doc looked enormously proud of himself. "See, Jane. Everything's all worked out and settled."

Jane Hornbeck didn't look pleased with the solutions offered, though. Not pleased at all.

CHAPTER 13

PILED-UP GREEN-BLACK THUNDERCLOUDS swept south-east across the mountain tops. From inside the clouds, intermittent blue-white flashes escaped, piercing the September afternoon sky. Thunder, long in arriving, echoed through the house, surrounding meadows and forest. Rain fell in spits and sputters.

"Just enough to spot the windows. Won't even wet down the dust, much less the grass and trees," Emmie grumped as she stood in the open back door, folding the last of the laundry she and Alexa had just rescued from the clothesline.

Alexa with Tiger in her lap, attempted to relax in the porch rocker. It was warm ... unseasonably warm, and she unbuttoned the top buttons of her dress and laid back the collar. No breeze moved the heavy oppressive air as she looked out across the small, ripe, brown meadow and into the forest beyond. There had been no measurable rain in the valley since June and the land lay bone-dry and baked. Among the trees, a resinous odor hung above a carpet of dead pine-needles, and the branch tips, their moisture evaporated, looked more gray than green.

"If we don't get some rain and soon, we're bound to burn this whole forest down," Emmie observed in a voice tinged with desperation. "Maybe even the house and barns."

"I've heard this is the worst dry spell they've ever had. Even worse than last year."

"Bill says if you put two years like these last two back-to-back, folks are gonna go broke." Emmie stood wringing her hands in the newly washed dishtowel she had folded and obviously forgotten about.

"I know the only good cut of hay we got was in July, and we're luckier than most. Both Bill and David say we can't get through the winter with the hay we have unless we sell most of the cattle. Means we won't have much stock to breed with for next year if we do that."

"Also means you won't get much money for your beef 'cause everyone else is in the same fix and selling right and left," Emmie reminded Alexa.

"I know," Alexa said with a deep sigh. This wasn't the way she had planned for things to go and even though it wasn't her fault, she still felt responsible for the state of the ranch affairs. She had only been saved from the impending ruin many of the other ranchers faced by the dedicated work of Jake and Bill, and the wise and loving advice given by David. She did miss David. He had spent much of the summer in Boise City working with the Idaho exhibit for the Columbian Exposition. Even made a couple of trips to Chicago over the matter. He had written faithfully, though, and she had a small stack of letters tied with a blue satin ribbon tucked carefully in her bureau drawer. These she read and reread each evening.

"When's Mister David expected back?" Emmie asked as though reading Alexa's mind.

"This weekend, I hope. He promised me he'd return in time to attend the social a week from

Wednesday to help Doc Ward's campaign for congress." Alexa doubted Doc Wad would win. Just as Helen had predicted, although the people liked him a great deal, he was getting only lip service as support from them. With the stock breeding that was going on, the ranchers kept Doc busy. He was too good a veterinarian for them to send him away deliberately. And Mrs. Hornbeck relied more and more on him for advice regarding her ranch since David's time and attention centered on the exhibit.

"They still gonna have that dinner, even if nobody plans on voting for Doc?"

"Most definitely. Haven't had a real social since the box social in June. With the drought, people feel a need to get together and share their misery. I know I do."

Alexa felt rather than saw the raging violence building inside the cloud as it changed in shape and size. It was grown enough now to block out the sun. The air cooled and the great cloud mass bulged ever higher into the sky. She watched it move slowly, steadily out over the forest toward Martin's mill.

Thinking of Martin, she reminded herself that she must ride over soon and let him know of the social. Things hadn't been going well for him, and he hadn't been to see her much lately. His logging operation ran on too slim a budget and major equipment failures, accidents, and labor problems took more and more of his time and attention.

The tension in the cloud broke. A jagged streak of white-hot lightning cracked between cloud and earth. A flash half-blinded her. The nearly instant thunder-clap indicated how close the strike had been and jarred through her and rattled the windows and dishes in the house. Now the cloud seemed no longer able to control the electrical charges, and they arced, flashed, and struck with abandon.

Emmie and Alexa watched the forward edge of the

154

massive cloud approach the slope of the mountain where Martin's crew worked. It seemed to pause a fraction of a second before loosing a bolt of lightning. Alexa saw the flash squarely and directly, and its serpentine image remained clearly on her retina as she blinked her eyes. Even in the interval between the strike and the accompanying thunder, the cloud seemed to have grown less theatening. It continued on its path across the mountains to the east, but with diluted menace.

"All passion spent," Alexa quoted softly aloud.

"You say something?" Emmie asked.

"No . . . no." Alexa stood, dumping Tiger unceremoniously onto the porch floor, and started for the barn. Maybe in her restless mood, a ride on Red would calm her.

Martin looked up at the darkening afternoon sky from the ridge he was riding along, a ridge well-covered by a fine forest of Douglas fir. The dark, nearly black bark absorbed the limited light and added to the mysterious aura of the deep timberland. From an open space, he paused to watch the ominous cloud. Its leading edge approached him, growing more menacing by the minute. Since he was only part-way up the slope, he wasn't concerned, knowing that lightning always strikes the tallest object. He dismounted King and stood, leaning against the trunk of an unpretentious fir to wait out the storm. Across the narrow steep canyon from him, he spotted a white pine, remarkably vigorous and healthy. Although the tallest tree in its immediate vicinity, it was much farther from the cloud than the trees on the ridge crest. The vigorous looking growth of that tree was no accident. Its roots undoubtedly tapped some underground water source. If the tree was higher on the ridge, its sharp growing-tip would offer an excellent attraction for lightning.

Then suddenly, a blue-white flash a few millionths of a second long poured between cloud and earth through the tree. A terrifying force spiraled up the sap channel just under the bark. Along this narrow channel the intense heat vaporized not only the sap, but the wood itself. The pressure build-up exploded. A long spiral weal rose from tip to root. Pieces of bark blew out and hurtled through the air. Deafening sounds of rending and explosion split the air and rolled as reverberating thunder through the canyon.

Martin sank against his backrest and gripped King's reins. The air filled with left-over electricity crackled around them. Martin felt his hair stand up and King reared, pawing the charged air. "Whoa, boy. Whoa," he crooned to the startled horse. Momentarily blinded by the brilliant bolt, Martin didn't dare move. King, although quivering from the shock, responded to Martin's voice and stood quiet. He continued to show his agitation, nonetheless, through his heavy breathing and short shrill whickerings.

When Martin could see again, he carefully scanned the tree. It appeared that little had changed by its ordeal. The most noticeable was its tip, lopped over like a wilting plant, and a faint tar-like odor that hung in the still air. A slight charred smell from the intense heat drifted toward him, but plentiful sap must have oozed in quickly and kept the wood from burning.

He sat, watching the tree for signs of smoke. He'd make the effort to cross the steep canyon if there seemed a need. The tinder-dry forest could ignite from even a tiny spark. He kept his vigil for a couple of hours, but even through binoculars, he could see no sign of smoke. It was growing late, and he would be caught in the forest at dark if he didn't start back. Even with the full moon for a candle, traveling at night was still dangerous. The country was cut with ravines whose sheer edges were camouflaged by trees and berry bushes, and the shadows made them still more deceptive.

"Come on, King. Let's get out of here. We'll come back up the other side tomorrow and make sure there's no fire alive in the tree."

Martin slept poorly that night as though anticipating the day to come. It began early with burned bacon and coffee that tasted like it had been brewed in the heel of an old boot. It was becoming increasingly obvious that Slim needed a weekend in town away from the cook shack.

Soon after breakfast, the wide leather belt that drove the saw slipped off its shaft. Turned into a deadly weapon, it narrowly missed the crew and flew spinning out of control until it slammed into a huge fir and collapsed in a tortured heap at the foot. The mill was then shut down for the remainder of the day while repairs were made.

Up the mountain where the crews were cutting, a new faller missed his spot when he jumped clear and broke his leg. By the time Martin got back from taking him to the doctor in town, it was too late to ride up and check on the lightning strike. He did walk to the top of the hill in back of the camp where he could look into the canyon beyond, but he could see no smoke. *Been more'n twenty-four hours. Most likely no damage has been done, or it would have been smoking by now*. The picture of the exploding bark nagged him though, and his hair again stood on end at the memory of the feeling of the charged air after the strike. *Guess I won't feel right 'til I make sure there's no live sparks. First thing in the morning, I'll ride up there.*

The evening after the storm found Alexa, at sunset, feeling the heat of another abnormally warm September day ebb away. The hot breeze died down, and the autumn haze shrank earthward, leaving her world cool and calm and clear. Unconsciously she raised her eyes to the ridge where the lightning had struck yesterday. She couldn't believe such a strike hadn't produced instant smoke, but there was no hint of where the violent bolt had hit.

"Well, Tiger, looks like we escaped a fire again. Wish we'd get rain or snow and put an end to this everlasting worry."

The light faded into early evening and Alexa, with Tiger in her arms, retreated from the chill into the warmth of the sitting room made cozy by a small crackling fire in the heating stove. Bill would soon be down from the bunkhouse for their evening discussion of ranch affairs, and Alexa needed to finish her ledgers.

David grew very aware of the smoke-filled valley as he rode in. Thank heaven, the smoke was from a big fire in Oregon that he had heard about. He had worried all week about the lightning storm that had passed over Idaho five days earlier. It caused numerous fires, but the Rathdrum area had apparently been spared. Nevertheless, he looked to his beloved mountains just in case. But the smoke, acrid to the nose, was too thick to see through.

Urging his horse into a cantor, he returned his thoughts to Boise City and Idaho's Exposition exhibit. Taking a shortcut in his haste to be home, he prepared to walk his horse through the small stream that ran across the corner of the Hornbeck ranch. His thoughts were jerked into the present when he discovered a pitiful trickle of water running through the gravelly bottom where a clear, flowing stream usually flowed. He hadn't been in the valley for nearly three weeks and the lack of moisture had obviously grown acute in his absence. He couldn't remember when this creek didn't flow and he had heard no stories of its drying up in the past. Anxious now, he prodded his horse into a faster gait and hurried to the ranch.

Martin couldn't sleep. Heavy smoke from the coast fires made him so nervous that the past three nights he had wakened in a cold sweat from nightmares of blazing forests. He got out of bed and looked out the window. He decided it was near enough to daylight to stay up and ride out to take a look into the canyon where he would see the strike. He hadn't been able to get up there since the storm six days ago. Perhaps seeing the spot would ease his mind and permit him to get some rest.

He crested one ridge just as the sun crested the other, but what he saw stopped his heart. The fire had eaten away from the base of the lightning-stricken tree and found a downed log about sixty or seventy feet long that it was consuming lazily. A pine cone had apparently caught fire and then rolled down the canyon spreading sparks as it went, for there was a strip of fire about thirty feet long downhill. The fire had only destroyed a clump of brush. No big trees were in its path. If he could get a crew up here fast, they could build a line around the fire and contain it swiftly with no damage to the forest. He wheeled King about and rode as quickly as the rough terrain would allow, back to camp for his men.

Despite their varied clothing, the loggers looked like a band of primitive warriors marching to battle, their double-bitted axes, shovels, and cross-saws carried over their shoulders like weapons for hand-to-hand combat. They strung out single-file along the narrow trail as Martin, as their chieftan, led the way. With two miles to travel, Martin set a brisk pace.

"There she is!" Martin yelled as he halted to re-evaluate the situation since he had left. The men crowded around him and looked into the canyon where a faint trace of smoke surrounded a denser column.

"Come on!" Martin thundered and plunged diagonally down the steep hillside through trees and brush in the shortest distance to the fire. He halted the men about twenty feet from where the smoke rose along the upper side of the log. Here they paused to catch their breath.

"We'll make a fire-line and let it burn itself out. A foot or two wide, free of duff will be enough. Flint, take your crew and get rid of any low-hanging branches, brush, or saplings that could go up along the line."

The men set to work with a great show of spirit accompanied by the usual lengthy string of curses that punctuated their speech. Martin left them and scouted the fire.

When he returned, five of the men were chopping up the big log that lay across their intended fire line. Seeing a third of his crew so occupied while most of the fire burned uncontrolled, Martin cursed them roundly and sent them to the upper end of the fire.

The autumn sun struck fiercely against the slope where they worked. The breeze fell off and an oven-like mid-morning calm lay in the canyon. The scraping and shoveling caused a fine dust to rise and it hung in the air, irritating throats and nostrils. The men grew tired. Their hands and faces, sooty and dusty, were streaked where sweat-beads rolled continuously down.

Martin stopped sawing limbs, assessed the crew's position, and realized they were making fine progress. At the rate they were going, the line should be closed in another hour. As though aware they were close to victory, the men sucked water from their canteens, grabbed quick bites from Slim's thick roast beef sandwiches, and continued their tasks, taking no real breaks.

Something changed and Martin looked about. The breeze came first as a little puff and then a long sigh as if a giant had been holding his breath. The smaller branches swayed gently. Wicks of flame wavered and spiraled, then leaned backward and stayed that way. For a moment, it seemed as if the wind might aid the warriors, blowing the flames back into the burn. The fresh breeze moved the stagnant air, cooled their faces and gave them smoke-free air to breathe. Then they remembered the other side of the fire. Instantly, what had been the front of the fire became its rear. Instead of advancing down-canyon where the crew worked, it shifted and took off up-canyon.

The speed with which it advanced wasn't great, but it moved much more rapidly than a tired crew could build a fire-line.

"She's outsmarted us!" Flint shouted.

Martin, sick at heart, stopped to weigh his alternatives. Either he could fall back well up-canyon and try to build a line across the front of the fire, or he could keep the crew where they were and try to narrow the front and gradually squeeze it off. He looked at the tired men and chose the safer strategy.

"We'll stay here and flank her, men. We'll catch her!" he said, with prayer in his heart. "This wind'll die down pretty soon." And if it didn't, he stood to lose all his forest and with that, the men, their jobs. They were all fighting for their lives against an enemy that knew no compassion or remorse, and fought to the death.

"Come on!" he yelled. "Let's get to work. We'll catch her on the up-side!" And with one Paul Bunyon-like ax-stroke, he cut clean through the butt of a young tree standing too close to the line.

Leaving the men working with renewed vigor, Martin again hiked to higher ground where he could see the scope of the fire. His practiced eye measured the distance. It had burned an area somewhat more than a quarter of a mile long. There was still a chance of controlling it, if he could get some fresh men to take over while his loggers ate and rested.

Surely someone in the valley had seen the smoke by

now and was coming with reinforcements. Martin looked at his pocket watch. The time since they had arrived had sped by and it was already after twelve o'clock. The sun didn't seem as hot as usual for noon. Looking skyward, he watched a thin white gauze of high clouds coming from the west dim the sun a trifle. Did this mean a chance of rain? If the clouds deepened and continued to cool the sun, the fire could cease to burn as hot this afternoon. Perhaps the Lord had heard his desperate prayer after all.

David couldn't sleep and rose early. Today he had to decide what to do with their cattle. It was down to how many cows they could keep and feed since their range was dried up and water scarce.

The house was still quiet when he finished dressing. From habit, as soon as he stepped outside, he surveyed the sky. A wind during the night had cleared the smoke from the valley, and he could see the last stars clearly in the pre-dawn sky. However, when he turned to the east his heart stopped. There, in the faint light, from the mountain behind Alexa's ranch rose a tall thin plume of smoke.

He decided too many days had passed for the fire to be have been caused by the storm. "Darn some careless logger!" David swore and broke into a run toward the bunkhouse. "May his soul rot for starting that fire!" He didn't need this sort of interruption to his plans. He had come home for one specific reason and when that was accomplished, he would be returning to Boise City and then on to Chicago.

Abruptly roused, the hands dressed quickly, all the while roundly cursing the fire and the party who had set it.

"Shall I ride for help?" someone asked.

"No need," David replied. "Soon as folks wake and spot it, they'll do just as we are. There'll be plenty of help in no time. Be sure to take all our cross-

162

cut saws, axes, and shovels," David reminded them. "Don't forget to fill your canteens. Don't count on the usual water supplies." Taking the cook aside, David instructed him to prepare lunches while the men wrangled their horses.

The dew had burned off by the time they were ready to leave, but the amount of smoke rising seemed to remain constant. Maybe he and his men were going to be in time to keep the fire from running away after all.

The terrain was rough and cut by canyons. This slowed their progress, making it late afternoon before David and his men arrived at the fire. The trail broke clear of the trees at the top of the ridge and they could look down on the fire-line.

Even believing the loggers had started the fire and angry as he was at them, David felt sorry for Martin's crew as they stood, dog-tired, grimy, and sweaty, leaning on their shovels watching the back-fires spring to life and go roaring toward the main fire. The flames were sucked along by the draft that the main fire pulled in toward itself.

David saw the head-on clash of the two fires as they piled together like two large waves ripping into each other. A clump of underbrush suddenly disappeared in white-yellow flames. Close by, a ninety-foot fir tree, its resins vaporized by the heat, exploded into a flame that towered at least a hundred feet upward. It issued a long-drawn hiss that stopped just short of a roar. For a few seconds the dying tree stood out, its needles a white-hot torch of flaming gas. The tips of its branches burned red for a moment, then the tree cooled and stood, reduced to a darkened silhouette of naked branches against the fire-lit sky.

David gave a shout to Martin who waved and came running to meet the fresh crew. "Pull your men out for a rest and we'll take over," David said. "I'm sure there'll be more help along soon."

Martin nodded and spread the word quickly through his crew. As the loggers fell back to rest, the warm dry breeze that had been blowing much of the day turned cool and damp. They tried to make themselves comfortable by building a fire in the burned area. Grown accustomed to the heat of the forest fire, now they were cold despite the campfire. And having eaten the last of their sandwiches long ago, they added hunger to the growing list of miseries.

Joining them, Martin said, "Feels like rain. What do your joints say, Cliff?"

"Say you're right," the old man answered as he sat near the fire rubbing his knees.

Martin tipped his head back and felt the first tiny drops splatter across his face. Breathing a silent prayer of thanksgiving, he lay down on the ground in the sooty ashes to sleep. He was nearly out when he heard an unmistakable 'crink-crunk-squinch' that signaled the coming of a pack train.

The little sprinkle of rain in the night hadn't amounted to anything. Growing increasingly anxious this morning, Alexa kept leaving her ledgers to look out the window at the column of smoke. It stayed much the same until mid-morning, then suddenly it changed shades of gray and increased noticeably in volume.

Seeking Emmie in the kitchen, Alexa found her stoically peeling potatoes. "Isn't there something we can do?" she wailed at Emmie, and reached for a potato to peel. "It's going to burn up our forest and here we sit, doing nothing."

"Nothing!" Emmie gestured with her hand toward the oven where she had roasts and hams baking. Pies cooled on all the tables and windowsills. And now she was making a large batch of potato salad.

"Who's going to eat all this food?" Alexa asked. "Are the fire fighters going to come back here? That is, if there is anyone up there."

164

"There's men up there, all right. Don't think an experienced lumber man like Martin's gonna let his forest go up in flames without a fight, do you?"

Alexa's reply was interrupted by the sound of a wagon coming up to the house. She rushed out the back door in time to welcome Jane Hornbeck as she pulled her buckboard to a halt next to the porch. This wasn't the fashionable lady Alexa knew. Rather, she was dressed in calico, a full matching apron, a poke bonnet, and drove the team with considerable expertise. Alexa's mouth fell open and she stood staring.

Mrs. Hornbeck climbed briskly from the wagon and hurried up the back steps. "Come, girl. Don't stand there gawking. We've got work to do. Your ranch is closest to the fire so it'll serve as a base camp. We'll load the food and blankets from here and take them to the men." When she walked into the kitchen, she paused and gaped. "I didn't think you'd have anything done. I owe you an apology."

"I've only been helping. Emmie gets the credit for knowing what to do," Alexa said, feeling young and useless.

Mrs. Hornbeck whipped off her bonnet, rolled up her sleeves, and began rinsing the newly peeled potatoes. "No matter who did it. It's done and that's what's important. Rest of the women should be coming right along with their things. Potato salad'll taste good to the men, Emmie." She turned to Alexa. "Is Jake around?"

"I think so."

"Go fetch him and bring him down here," Jane Hornbeck ordered. All the soft lady-like manners were gone and in their place a hard-working knowledgeable ranch woman.

As she ran to the barn, thankful to be free of the kitchen, Alexa wondered if David had ever seen his mother like this. If he had, he surely wouldn't fuss and worry over her like he did.

When the corrals came into view, she was surprised to see mules barricaded inside and packing boxes stacked against the barn. Jake was busy stringing harnesses over the fence. "What are you doing with all those mules?" she asked.

"Neighbors brought 'em over. Gonna make a pack-string to take supplies into the fire fighters."

"You're not planning to make such a trip, I hope. I need you here a lot worse than they need you there."

Jake looked uncomfortable. "Nope. Me'n Bill had that out this morning. He says the same as you, so he's taking the train. But he don't know the lay of the land like I do. What if he gets lost?" Jake obviously wasn't giving up without one last try.

"I imagine with all the cattle herding Bill's done this summer, he knows the country enough not to get lost. Mrs. Hornbeck's here and wants you down at the house," Alexa said.

Jake's look turned sour. "I thought I was through dancing for that bossy old woman. You tell her I got things to do at the barn."

"I will not. I imagine what she wants is equally as important as what you have to do here."

"What she wants is to tell me how to put a pack-train together as if I didn't know after forty years of 'doin'it,'" Jake retorted. But he dropped the harness he was holding and joined Alexa in the walk back to the house.

The yard in front of the house was full of wagons when they arrived.

Jake recognized the two old men lounging near the front steps and hobbled over to them.

Alexa started in the kitchen door, but the room was so full of women packing boxes and crates with food, she felt in the way. Jane Hornbeck spotted her, though, and came quickly through the crowd.

"Did you get Jake?"

Alexa nodded and pointed. Mrs. Hornbeck bustled

166

down the porch to where the men were visiting. "You men! Take my wagon load down to the barn and start filling the pack boxes. Move now, and don't dawdle. We've hungry, tired men up on that fire. It's up to us to get them supplies." Coming back to where Alexa stood, she said, "You start driving these other wagons up to the barn and help put the supplies in the boxes. Bring back the first empty wagon, and we'll be ready to load the food you have here." She paused to look at the jeweled watch pinned to her dress. "Should have that train on its way by three o'clock."

Alexa, at last feeling useful, untied the horses of the closest wagon and climbed in. Much as the cause of the excitement distressed her, she found herself being drawn into the action surrounding her and relishing the diversion. She wondered briefly if Martin and David felt the same stimulation.

CHAPTER 14

THE FIRE HAD RAGED ITS DESTRUCTION for three days now, and an overwhelming sense of defeat and fear hovered over the gathering of the faithful in the little wooden building being used as a temporary church. The itinerant preacher in his long prayer added a simple petition "for those loved ones who are struggling to save our livelihood and our forest, and who may be, this day, in danger." He had hardly finished and announced his text when one of Jake's elderly friends slipped quietly up the aisle and whispered to the organist, his employer.

Her neighbors bent close to hear and then a wave of whispers spread outward. People leaned across pews to get the message. No one was listening to the sermon, and the preacher, a sensible man and curious as the rest, stopped talking and motioned to the organist to come up and tell him the news. Then he cleared his throat.

"Apparently the battle to control the fire has been lost and word has been brought to us that it rages out of control and some of our men are thought to be trapped."

Gasps of dismay issued from those to whom this was news. The rest sat in stricken silence. Alexa felt her heart race, stop, and then beat an irregular pattern that made breathing difficult. Were any of the men David and Martin? *Oh, Lord, please don't let it be them*. Then, embarrassed at her selfishness, prayed, *Forgive me, Lord, for thinking only of myself. Please let all who have labored so long and diligently be safe*.

The preacher, a wise man, said, "Let us join in singing 'Praise God from whom all blessings flow,' after which, considering the circumstances, I shall pronounce the benediction and dismiss you to go to your homes. There I hope you can find comfort and peace in communion with the Lord until we are brought happier news."

When the people stepped outside, they were horrified to see that the column of gray smoke had grown to huge proportions during the short time they had been there. Alexa and Emmie wasted no time in visiting but hurried straight to their buggy.

"Alexa," Jane Hornbeck called. "Won't you come stay with me? A number of the ladies who's husbands are at the fire are coming over."

"Thanks for asking, but my land's burning and I feel a need to be there." She was sure Mrs. Hornbeck didn't understand that when Alexa looked at the fire destroying Martin's timber and her ranch, she felt personally violated and powerless to fight back. She needed solitude in which to face the knowledge that Martin and David might be dead. She didn't want to turn her agony into a public death watch complete with weeping and the wringing of hands. All she wanted was to saddle Red and ride alone to a high ridge from which to watch her ruin. Then she remembered Emmie. "Would you like to join the women?"

"No." In a voice thick with tears, Emmie asked. "Did you know Bill went to the fire this morning. He

169

took another train of food in and medical supplies. Took Doc Ward with him."

"Bill! Oh, Emmie, I am sorry."

Emmie only shrugged and continued knotting and unknotting her handkerchief. Alexa sat a moment wondering if she should tell Jane Hornbeck about Doc Ward. Then she decided Mrs. Hornbeck had enough to bear knowing David might be trapped. She didn't need to hear of Doc's whereabouts as well.

Alexa and Emmie drove home in silence, their eyes glued to the towering plume of smoke in front of them. Once home, she changed into her riding clothes, grabbed Uncle Clyde's binoculars, and ran to the barn, stopping only long enough to give Red a whistle. He responded immediately and by the time she arrived, she stood at the barn door, nickering and blowing. "Good boy," she said and gave him the expected lump of sugar. Carrying lumps of sugar was infinitely easier than packing around oats to serve as Red's reward.

Entering the barn on her way to get her saddle and bridle, she stopped short. There sat Jake on a saw horse, shoulders hunched forward and head bowed, watching the chickens. "Jake?" she called softly.

Without looking at her, he asked, "Where you going Miss Alexa?"

"If my trees are going to burn, I'm want to be there to see them."

"Need to get up high for that," he said in a tired voice. "Best take Molly. She's more sure-footed than Red, and she won't shy if you get too close to the fire."

"What about that bone-wracking trot?"

"I think you're in the mood to take that out of her today," he said and raised his head for the first time to look at Alexa through sad eyes.

"You're right about that," Alexa said grimly and grabbed the tack.

170

"I'll whistle her in for you," Jake offered and with obvious effort and pain made his way outside. "Sure do wish I was going with you. Mighty hard having to sit and wait while others is taking the action."

"I don't think there's much action. From the looks of the smoke, things are completely out of control. You've served well by taking care of the pack-trains, Jake. Couldn't have fed and bedded all those men without you." She put her arm around his shoulder and hugged him.

All the while Alexa saddled Molly, she talked to her, warning Molly of the consequences if she tried her famous trot. Alexa swung into the saddle and signalled her to start. Off she went, not having given any heed to Alexa's words. Alexa raked Molly with the rowels of her spurs and the stunned horse leaped into a full gallop. Alexa pulled Molly up after a short distance. She didn't want the horse winded and tired to begin the strenuous trip. "Now, are you ready to behave and walk like a lady?" Alexa demanded.

Again when Alexa gave Molly the signal to go, the horse started into the trot, but Alexa pulled back firmly on the reins and Molly settled at once into a rhythmic walk. "Good girl," Alexa said and patted the little mare's neck. "We're going to get along fine."

Alexa rode the familiar trail to the deserted logging camp and then followed the now well-worn path made by the pack-trains into the hills. The trail led up and up, lurching and twisting through the forested mountains. Tall fir trees overhung the path dimming the light until she broke free of boughs on the ridge crest. Here she stopped to let Molly blow a bit and watch the smoke, varied shades of gray full of whorls and convolutions filling the sky above her. The sun, high overhead, shone as a red disk through the dense smoke. Although Alexa still cast a shadow, the light had changed to an ominous yellow. Bits of feathery ash settled over her, and her nostrils felt parched from the smoke and hot dry wind that blew toward her.

She hadn't brought a canteen and realized she had been foolish. She had heard how the water sources had dried up. Still, she hoped she might find a spring this high up so she kept looking as she rode along. At last, off the trail through the trees, she could see a clearing. Dismounting, Alexa walked through the underbrush to a lovely little glade set like an emerald at the foot of a cliff. She stepped into a tiny enchanted world. A small, crystal-clear stream fed from springs in the cliff, dropped in gentle falls over glistening rocks from pool to shimmering pool. The rocks above the pools were covered with deep cushion moss kept always green by the dainty spray from the miniature waterfalls. Farther back from the stream, where the air was still moist, ferns grew, delicate and lush. The air was filled with delightful perfumed scents of colorful wildflowers. Out of the carpet of ferns and meadow grass, red-brown fluted trunks of red cedars rose, and high overhead, the lacy canopy of branches let the sunlight penetrate through in long rays.

The glade was cool and the air, quiet. Alexa took off her hat, and stepping carefully among the ferns so as not to break any fronds, crossed the opening and knelt by the stream. The water was so clear that the tiny sprigs of algae in it seemed to be suspended in space. Small rainbow trout darted away when she leaned over to drink.

Her thirst satisfied, she stood and gazed about. Alexa prayed Martin and David had found a safe spot, and refused to think harm had come to any of the crews. As she breathed deeply from air not yet contaminated, she gave thanks for these few minutes of peace before she watered Molly, swung into the saddle, and started on.

By late afternoon, Alexa reached high spot along the ridge, where she could look full on the fire.

Through the smoke she could barely make out the far ridges, blackened and fire-swept. Below her in the canyon, the whole forest blazed. As she watched, a gust of wind struck, sending the fire forward. It engulfed a clump of young trees and she saw the flames shoot up. Heat, driven by the wind, beat against her face as it swept up-slope. And then the fire advanced into a stand of regal Douglas firs.

She remembered her grief at man's slaying of one of the beauties. But she had been able to partially accept the destruction when Martin explained the uses man made of the fine lumber. This wanton destruction filled her with rage, and her heart grew sick over the useless burning.

Alexa dismounted and settled down to watch. As the fire entered the thicker forest, it began to show a difference. Instead of the steady consuming creep, now it acted like a furnace, the tremendous heat drying out the needles, and then igniting a large section of the magnificent tree tops. With a deep roar—*like a freight train passing in the night*, Alexa thought—flames and dark smoke rose hundreds of feet, carrying blazing twigs, needles, and strips of bark up with it.

Having established a crown-fire, the dry canyon wind sent the fire toward Alexa at a steady rate. One tree after another disappeared with a deep hiss into a towering column of flame. For about a half a minute the hiss deepened into a roar. The burning boughs tossed as though blown by a hard wind. Then as the tree burned out, the roar faded.

But the heat had already dried the neighboring trees and they immediately towered in flaming ruin. As the crown-fire moved up the ridge, the great pines and fires burned like stalks of wheat in a field fire, only these flames leaped up hundreds of feet.

Alexa wet her lips parched by the heat, but they grew drier still, and cracked. She looked up to see a great rush of air wildly toss the high branches growing over her head. The tree-tops bent nearly double as powerful air currents clashed in a gigantic swirl. They tore bits of bark, needles, and rotten wood, swirled the litter upward and hurled it away. Dense smoke suddenly engulfed her and obscured her view. A strip of burning bark fell a short distance from her and the forest, dry as well-kept gun powder, flared instantly.

She started toward the spot fire. It was so small, she felt confident she could stamp it out, but at Molly's shrill neigh, Alexa turned. Burning debris was falling all around and igniting the duff. Flames flared into bushes and low branches and raced across the carpet of dry needles. Suddenly, smoke and fire sprang up all around her.

Alexa ran to where Molly, tied to a branch, trembled and shied from the fire. "Come, girl. Stay calm and we'll get out of here." Grabbing Molly's reins, Alexa ran back down the trail until a piece of burning branch fell on Molly's rump. She let out a terrified neigh, lunged free of Alexa, and plunged down the smoke-filled path out of sight.

Thick smoke blew out along the ground, flat before the wind. Alexa coughed and choked with it, and her eyes watered and stung. The air, furnace-hot, seared her lungs and throat. Smoke shut out the sun and she could only keep her direction by feeling the downhill slope.

The parching wind sucked the last memory of moisture from the fir forest and the pall of smoke hung, an impenetrable curtain. She lost the trail and began fighting her way through the brush and dense timber. Her run became a shuffle as she bent to catch the slightly cleaner air near the ground. All worry about Martin's and David's safety fled. She began praying harder than at anytime in her life for her own survival.

Then, directly ahead through the smoke, she saw

the glowing red-hot branches of a bush. Sparks from behind came sailing past letting her know it was useless going back. Left with no alternative, she went on through the blinding smoke toward the glowing branches. The bush was scarcely burning along its windward side. She looked about. Fire was everywhere. Here was the only way out. She threw her hands over her head, drew a deep breath, and dashed past the bush and the line of fire. Safely through, she slapped frantically at the burning spots on her clothes and wiggled her feet, uncomfortably warm in the hot shoes.

She seemed to be in a small clearing covered with meadow grass and ferns. Keeping low to the ground, she explored her tiny fire-guarded prison. The smoke was so dense she nearly stepped in the stream. "Oh!" she exclaimed as she realized she was in the little glade she had explored earlier. "Thank you, Lord," she breathed aloud.

Several deer, trying to out-run the fire, bounded through the clearing, startling her. Alexa pushed aside the charred wind-strewn debris covering the water and drank her fill. Then she took off her shoes and waded into the deepest of the pools and lay down. Her heart pounded with terror as the forest around her erupted with a roar into a crowning fire. A brown bear lumbered past, oblivious to her presence.

She kept her head low against the water where the air was cooler. However, she continued to cough from the thick smoke and pant from the effort. The pool was too shallow to cover her so she turned from side to side to keep her clothes wet and extinguish any undetected sparks.

A hideous screaming hiss rose from the forest floor and swept over the little glade. Her world turned a flaming yellow-orange as the fire rose over the small sanctuary. A searing blast of heat accompanied the fire. She snatched a quick breath, held it, and thrust her head under the water. When her lungs felt near to bursting, she surfaced and shivered as the inferno raced on.

Earlier, Alexa had observed islands of forest untouched except for the withering heat. By some miracle, it had left another such little island of forest, her tiny glade.

Alexa lay trembling from the shock of having escaped. Her teeth chattered and when she tried to stand, her knees refused to hold her. Crawling out onto the bank, she sat among the heat-shriveled ferns and wept.

At last she cried, wondering if Molly had escaped. How many of the men fighting the fire had experienced what she had just gone through, only not been so forunate? She sat for a very long time staring at the ruin around her. What had been beautiful, productive, full of life, now was a place of desolation, ugliness, and death. Martin's forest stood burned and useless, and her's would soon be left the same way.

The wind cleared the air, blowing the smoke before the fire. She could look up through the standing black skeletons of once mighty trees and see gray cloud-patched sky. With its dunking, her watch failed to run—she could only guess the time. Late afternoon she decided. It was much too late to try walking back to the logging camp so she prepared to spend the night. Unfortunately, there was little to prepare. No delicate boughs were left to soften the ground. The best she could do was clear the sooty duff from under a once glorious cedar and curl into the untidy burrow.

Using a short flat stick, she began scratching away layers of long dead needles. The crude tool turned her work into an arduous chore. Her arms grew tired and she was forced to rest often.

The unexpected cracking sounds of branches and twigs caused her to pause and look up. There, standing at the edge of the clearing, was David, his

176

face black with soot and smoke, and smeared on his cheeks where he had wiped it.

"David!" She scarcely recognized the rough scratchy croak issuing from her heat-seared throat. Leaping up, she ran to him and they fell into each other's arms. She looked into his blood-shot eyes, which shone out of the blackness of his face with a strange glare. One shirt sleeve was gone and dried blood crusted over a long ugly gash. Holes were burned in his shirt and his hat was gone. He limped as he walked with her to the stream's edge.

Still without speaking, he dropped to his knees and drank thirstily from the ash-covered water. His thirst finally satisfied, Alexa helped him remove his scarred boots and he plunged blistered feet into the cool water. He tried to talk but no sound would come forth. She lip-read, "Martin's trapped." Learning that, she curled into David's arms and sobbed. Mutely they shared the horror each had survived.

It was late afternoon when Martin set the first back-fire to take advantage of the switch in the wind direction. Two loggers jumped in and took care of a point of fire that jumped the hastily cleared fire line. As they came running out, their shirts steaming, Martin lit the next stretch of back-fire and on the other side of the line, David did the same. Between the two back-fires, the danger was great. Constantly checking behind himself to make sure no men were left, Martin continued to thrust his blazing torch into dead leaves and fallen branches.

With a few miracles, they might even hold the fire tonight. A billowing curl of smoke circled him, and he coughed and shut his eyes. Sparks lit on his shirt sleeve and he slapped them out. As he stepped away from the heat of the last back-fire, a long warning whoop came from behind him.

Martin swung around. "Run, men!" he shouted.

Flinging his torch into the bushes, he joined them in flight. "Where's David?" he asked of no one in particular.

The fleeing men either didn't hear him or didn't know, for they kept running without answering. Martin turned and looked frantically through the rising smoke and flames. "David!" he shouted repeatedly. At last, receiving no answer and finding the heat rapidly growing unbearable, he also ran.

It was hot and smoky and Martin was soon panting hard. The fire spread across the fire-line. It erupted out of control and quickly spread of its own accord. Martin was trapped.

He stopped, blowing hard. He had been in too many tight places in his life to panic. Upon closer examination, things didn't look too bad ahead. He wrapped his bandana over his nose and mouth, pulled his felt hat low, took a deep breath, and dashed along the line into the fire.

The first few leaps were bad. Flames grasped at him and searing hot smoke swirled around him. Just as he wondered if he was going to survive, he came out into an open space. He fell down and rubbed his smoking clothes with dirt. Then he was up and dashing through another bad spot ahead.

The next hole turned out better than he had hoped. He was in brush and away from the thick-growing trees, but as he ran up the steep canyon, blood pounded hard in his ears from the effort and strain. His legs felt like they had lead bolts attached. His chest tightened against the smoke-thickened air as he struggled upward. He climbed another hundred feet before his heart began pounding so violently he had to stop for breath. Looking to the right, he saw a point of fire running almost even with him.

He plunged ahead once more. Just when he felt he could go no farther, he came to a cleared place . . . a deer trail perhaps . . . and now he followed the switch-backs up the steep canyonside. Swirling, suffocating smoke impeded his progress, forcing him to bend low to the ground for air. He grew so weary it took all his determination to keep forging ahead. At last, his throat and lungs burned unbearably from the smoke and coughing, he was forced to rest.

Leaning against a snag, he attempted to catch his breath and ease the pain. Over the crackling hiss of the fire, he thought he heard the terror-stricken neighing of a horse. He listened intently. There it was again! Just off the trail above him. Quickly scrambling around the rocks, Martin dived into a thick clump of young trees. Beyond, he could see flames licking at the outer edges of the fine timber and rearing frantically in the middle was Molly, her reins hopelessly snared by the underbrush.

While he freed the horse, his thoughts raced. What was Molly doing here wearing the saddle Alexa always used? *Oh, dear Lord, please don't let Alexa be out in this*, he prayed. But his mind wouldn't be stilled and he knew she had come to watch her trees burn. First David and now Alexa. These thoughts sickened him so, he leaned against the trembling Molly and silent tears slid down sooty cheeks and dripped unnoticed onto his shirt front.

"Oh, Alexa," he moaned. "Lord, help me to find her. Speak to me and lead me," he prayed softly.

"Come, Molly." He led the over-wrought horse up the final twists and turns to the top of the ridge. Once there, Martin found everything aflame in front of him. "We're going to have to wait it out, Molly. Can't go through that wall of fire." He sank down against a tree trunk, bowed his head to block the sight of the raging insatiable monster that refused to be stopped, and tried not to think of Alexa's whereabouts. Words from Jeremiah came to him . . . "I will kindle a fire in the forest and it shall devour all things round about it." It gave him no comfort at all, but a consoling passage would not come to mind.

Finally, the ground grew cool enough to walk on. Leading Molly, Martin, numb with grief and exhaustion, stumbled uncertainly along the trail that would eventually lead to the logging camp.

Tearing a strip of cloth from the tail of her shirtwaist, Alexa washed David's arm. "The cut is at least clean. In the morning when we get back to the ranch, we'll tend it properly."

David still lay, eyes closed. "Thank you, Alexa," he whispered.

"You're welcome," she answered softly. After making him as comfortable as possible, she asked, "What did you mean to say about Martin?"

David shuddered. "I think he was trapped by the back-fire we were setting. I heard him shouting, but I couldn't get across the line to help him."

Alexa lapsed into silence, trying to absorb the horror. Gradually, muted hoof beats entered the silence. "Molly!" Alexa leaped to her feet and ran back up the trail toward the sound. To her amazement, there coming toward her through the fading light were Martin and Molly.

"Martin!" Alexa cried. "Oh, Martin. We thought you'd been trapped in the fire. And you've found Molly." She threw her arms around him.

But he pushed her from him. "And you, my foolish girl . . . what are you even doing up here? I didn't think you'd behave so irresponsibly."

She looked quickly into his face to see tears seep over the rims of his eyes and down his cheeks, taking the sting from his words.

"I'm sorry. I had no idea how deadly a fire could be."

They entered the glade together and joined David. The two men recounted how they had escaped the fire.

"Isn't there anything that can stop it?" Alexa asked.

Martin sank down beside David. "Nothing man can do. We're left with prayer. When the Lord decides enough is enough, he'll put it out."

"Then, it seems we ought to pray," Alexa said.

The two men rose to their knees and Alexa knelt between them. David prayed first, then Alexa added her plea, and Martin concluded their petitions. They remained kneeling in silence, too weary and heartsick to move.

The cool breeze drove them to the cliff where they found shelter under an overhanging rock. They huddled together, miserable in the cold and dirt, and finally fell into an exhausted sleep.

Sometime in the early morning Alexa stirred against the protective grip of Martin and David. She was damp and cold. Becoming increasingly alert, she now recognized a familiar plop-plop-plop. Rain! Quiet, unhurried, sure, like a spoken promise from God that life and her world would go on.

CHAPTER 15

ALEXA STOOD IN FRONT OF THE LONG MIRROR , carefully examining her appearance. Even after three days and numerous scrubbings, she thought she could still see soot in the pores of her face and neck. *I'm going to be marked for life*, she decided mournfully.

She deliberately concentrated on the insignificant because she wasn't able to cope with the loss of her cattle herd just yet. Bill reported to her this morning that they had gotten through the one small section of the fence not yet re-built and onto Martin's land. The entire herd had been wiped out and with it, her only source of income.

A firm knock at the front door interrupted her dismal thoughts, and glad for another excuse to postpone facing her ruinous problems, she ran quickly to answer it.

She flung open the large door to find David, dressed in his finest clothes, nervously shaping and re-shaping his hat. "Why, David!" she gasped, nearly speechless with surprise.

"I do wish to apologize for calling at such an early hour and without warning," he stammered.

What on earth can he want that would cause him such anxiety?

"May I come in?" he asked shyly.

"Y—y—yes, of course," Alexa managed, and stepped into the hallway to let him pass. "Will you join me in the parlor?" she asked, her poise restored.

"Thank you," he murmured and followed her into the shade-darkened room.

Before joining David on the couch, Alexa quickly raised the shades and let the cloud-filtered light in.

"I know I have put you at a disadvantage, coming this way, but I have much to say to you and little time left before I must return to Boise City."

"What news do you bring from the capital?"

"Not a great deal that affects this area. The problems with the Coeur d'Alene miners are at last resolved and they are back at work. I also learned that the true train robbers have been caught which means Emmie's husband really didn't commit the crimes he was accused of."

David imparted the information casually, catching Alexa completely off-guard. She wanted to run to the kitchen at once and tell Emmie the good news, but etiquette prevented such a spontaneous reaction. Instead, Alexa said calmly, "The plans for the exhibit are coming well, I take it."

"Very well. I leave for Chicago next week where we will be choosing the lot on which to build the Idaho House. The design is completed and many of my suggestions have been incorporated."

Excitement radiated from him and she became caught up in his enthusiasm. "Tell me about it."

"Twenty thousand dollars have been appropriated for our exhibit. A most generous amount with which to work. Our theme is "Idaho—The Switzerland of America," and we are going to construct our house in the Swiss style, entirely of logs set on a basaltic rock and lava foundation. All the building materials are to be shipped to Chicago from Idaho. The main reception room will represent a hunter's cabin with a rock fireplace. I suggested we have the andirons made from two immense bear traps."

"It sounds so captivating. How I'd love to see it."

"You would?"

"Of course I would. It's going to be the most exciting event of my lifetime . It's hard to even imagine anything so grand."

David took her hand between his two cold ones. "Then, Alexa, my dearest heart, marry me, and you shall see it for our honeymoon."

Alexa sat stunned. Her brain whirled and she felt slightly giddy. She had dreamed of, but never really expected, his proposal. And now . . . "What about your mother?" was all she could think of to say.

"Mother's fine. She and Doc Ward are going to announce their own marriage plans immediately after the election. He'll take splendid care of her and the ranch. I'm free to leave this beautiful, but confining little valley and seek the challenges and adventure I crave. And I most desperately want you by my side, love."

And still Alexa hesitated. What was the matter with her? "Th—th— this is so sudden," she said lamely.

"Of necessity it is, and I apologize. But I learned only last week that I was being sent to Chicago. It seemed such a splendid trip for a honeymoon, I hurried home to ask you to marry me."

"How long would we stay there?"

"Since I'm to over-see the building and decorating of the house, I would suspect we would be there most of next year. After that, who knows?" He smiled that slow, dazzling smile that always flustered her thoroughly.

"David, may I have a couple of days to ponder it? With the fire and all, I just can't seem to think straight, and you're asking me not only to marry you, but to give up the ranch and leave Rathdrum. These are two very large decisions that I must sort out.''

''Mother would happily buy your ranch. She's been looking to expand her holdings for a long time. You have no problem there. I can understand your need to dwell a bit on such matters, but I am working against a dead-line. Do you have any idea when may I expect an answer?''

''Tomorrow,'' she said firmly. ''I will let you know tomorrow.''

At the door, Alexa found herself in David's arms. He studied her face intently. ''I do love you, my Alexa. I will be a good husband,'' he said before he bent and kissed her tenderly.

David's proposal bothered her terribly, but she didn't feel able to examine its uprooting effects on her life just yet. She stood on the porch and watched until she could no longer see him, then dashed to the kitchen to tell Emmie the news about the train robbers. Emmie's reaction wasn't what Alexa had expected.

''Don't take no stock in hearsay,'' Emmie said in a stiff voice.

''But Emmie, David heard it in Boise City. He wouldn't tell an untruth about something so important.''

''Won't believe a word until I have proof it's true.'' Emmie, her mouth set in a stubborn line, continued about the business of preparing dinner.

''What constitutes proof to you?'' Alexa asked, frustrated with Emmie's behavior.

''Word from the Sheriff in Boise City.''

''Very well, get your cloak and bonnet. We're going to town to the telegraph office.'' Alexa, grateful for something that required action instead of thinking, slipped into her gray, wool cloak and rushed out the door on her way to hitch up the buggy.

The Rathdrum telegraph office was a busy place this

185

morning. In fact, there were so many horses and pack animals tied to the hitching post, Alexa stopped down the street and she and Emmie had to walk back. Emmie was so anxious, she fairly flew along the street. Alexa gave up trying to stay with her, and slowed her pace to a saunter, eyeing the horses as she walked past.

Suddenly, she stopped. There stood King with a pack-horse tied to his saddle. Martin was leaving! And without saying goodbye. Alexa's heart dropped into her shoes. She hadn't realized how much she had grown to depend on him until now, and the thought that he would just ride away without a word left her paralyzed. She still hadn't recovered from her shock when he strode out of the telegraph office. His head bent while he read a piece of paper, he failed to see her and nearly knocked her down in his haste.

He grabbed wildly to save them both from a public tumble. "Alexa!" he gasped. "I'm sorry."

"Sorry isn't good enough. What do you mean riding away without saying so much as a by-your-leave? How dare you, Martin Taylor!" she fumed.

Martin took her arm and escorted her around the corner of the main street. "Alexa, I know I should have come by, but I couldn't face saying goodbye. I . . . just couldn't," he ended feebly.

Alexa looked carefully into his eyes and saw a gentleness, a tender caring he couldn't hide. "Martin, all my cattle are destroyed and Mrs. Hornbeck wants to buy the ranch. I don't know what to do." She felt his arms slip around her and he enfolded her to him. Resting against him, she drew strength from his giving spirit. "How is it? You always make things seem better," she whispered.

They remained thus, looking at each other, their eyes speaking a private language they both understood. They stayed that way until the giving became mutual, saying no word, yet both become more and more aware of the deep bond that had grown between them over the past months.

"Let's get away from here," Martin said in a husky whisper. Taking her arm, he guided her back onto the main street to get the horses.

As they passed the telegraph office, Emmie came flying out waving her telegram. "It's true! It's true! My Luke's a free man," she said through streaming tears.

Alexa embraced the happy woman. "Emmie, that's wonderful news. You must go to him at once."

Martin handed Emmie the reins. "Here, Emmie. Take the buggy. I'll see Alexa gets home."

Martin and Alexa walked slowly to the edge of town where a clear stream flowed. She sat on the bank and he sat down near her. "Seems we've sat like this before," he said softly.

They stayed all afternoon, talking, listening to the silvery bell-sounds of the river, watching eagles soar high overhead. Then, they hardly talked at all. There wasn't much to say. There was too much to say. Her pride wouldn't ask him to stay and since he had lost everything, his pride wouldn't let him.

The sun sank low and it grew chilly. "We'd better get you home before you freeze," he said.

Her arms firmly around his waist and her cheek pressed tightly against the firm muscles of his shoulder, they rode double back to the ranch. Emmie, her face aglow, greeted them as they entered the kitchen. Bill was lounging comfortably against the wall, watching Emmie prepare supper.

Emmie broke into a wide grin. "Like you both to meet my husband, Luke," she said proudly and crossed the kitchen to stand with him.

Alexa looked from one to the other, too stunned to speak. "Bill, you're Luke?" Laughter filled the room, and Alexa and Martin joined in hugging the happy couple.

"Martin, at least say you'll stay for supper and spend the night," Alexa urged. "You can sleep in the bunkhouse. Plenty of room there with Bill moving down here 'til we can get a house built."

Luke and Emmie looked delighted at the suggestion. "Just fixin' to spread the table. Got plenty," Emmie said.

They ate a simple, filling meal. During supper, the men talked of the prospects for Alexa's ranch.

"Without cattle and that good fence nearly finished, you could take up horse breeding. You got good stock in the valley to mix with. Could turn a fair profit, I'm thinking," Martin said.

"Ever thought of settling down and trying it yourself?" Luke asked Martin.

"Guess not. When the traveling life gets in the blood, you get used to looking for the crest of the next hill," Martin said, staring into the flames of the kerosene lantern on the table.

"Ever find it?" Luke asked. "Ever find what you was searching for?"

Alexa slipped away from the table and walked quickly down the hall and into the dark parlor. She heard Martin's steps and fought back the tears, trying to wipe them away. As he reached her, she turned to face him, feeling foolish and childish and embarrassed all at once. He came and took her by the shoulders. Tears insisted this time and Alexa couldn't hold them back. He pulled her to him, her forehead against his chest. She wrapped her arms tight around his body and felt his arms holding her securely to him. They stood entwined for a long time before Martin spoke.

"I've tried to put you out of my mind, night after night. Tried to tell myself we had nothing in common, that I didn't want to be tied to one piece of land. But I don't seem to lie well, even to myself."

She gave a little laugh and looked up into his face.

He took a deep breath and she could feel the rise of

his chest. "I do love you, Alexa . . . with all my heart. I have nothing to offer you but a burned-out lumber operation. And love enough to last several lifetimes."

"And I love you. We've got your land and my ranch. We're strong and full of dreams. With God's help, we'll build something wonderful here— together."

He touched her lips with his fingers and caressed her cheek, then bent over her, taking her lips in a warm loving kiss full of the promises of the good things to come.

ABOUT THE AUTHOR

MARYN LANGER is a delightful lady, crammed
with creativity. So full of fancy and tall tales is she
that one would never suspect she spends her days
teaching math to classrooms of children, nor that she
has written textbooks in her chosen field. She con-
fesses, however, that her mind, whether asleep or
awake, cannot help creating wonderful characters
from the past whose lives reflect her own strong
Christian faith and fortitude.

Mrs. Langer resides with her husband in Albion,
Idaho. MOON FOR A CANDLE is her second work
of romantic fiction, following WAIT FOR THE SUN.

A Letter To Our Readers

Dear Reader:

Pioneering is an exhilarating experience, filled with opportunities for exploring new frontiers. The Zondervan Corporation is proud to be the first major publisher to launch a series of inspirational romances designed to inspire and uplift as well as to provide wholesome entertainment. In order that we might better contribute to your reading enjoyment, we would appreciate your taking a few minutes to respond to the following questions and return to:

> Anne Severance, Editor
> The Zondervan Publishing House
> 1415 Lake Drive, S.E.
> Grand Rapids, Michigan   49506

1. Did you enjoy reading MOON FOR A CANDLE?

   ☐ Very much. I would like to see more books by this author!
   ☐ Moderately
   ☐ I would have enjoyed it more if _____

2. Where did you purchase this book? _____

3. What influenced your decision to purchase this book?

   ☐ Cover   ☐ Back cover copy
   ☐ Title   ☐ Friends
   ☐ Publicity   ☐ Other _____

4. Please rate the following elements from 1 (poor) to 10 (superior).

☐ Heroine   ☐ Plot
☐ Hero   ☐ Inspirational theme
☐ Setting   ☐ Secondary characters

5. Which settings would you like to see in future Serenade/Saga Books?

_____   _____

_____   _____

6. What are some inspirational themes you would like to see treated in future books?

_____   _____

_____   _____

7. Would you be interested in reading other Serenade/Serenata or Serenade/Saga Books?

☐ Very interested
☐ Moderately interested
☐ Not interested

8. Please indicate your age range:

☐ Under 18   ☐ 25–34   ☐ 46–55
☐ 18–24   ☐ 35–45   ☐ Over 55

9. Would you be interested in a Serenade book club? If so, please give us your name and address:

Name _____

Occupation _____

Address _____

City _____ State _____ Zip _____

Serenade Serenata Books are inspirational romances in contemporary settings, designed to bring you a joyful, heart-lifting reading experience.

Serenade Serenata books available in your local bookstore:

#1 ON WINGS OF LOVE, Elaine L. Schulte
#2 LOVE'S SWEET PROMISE,
      Susan C. Feldhake
#3 FOR LOVE ALONE, Susan C. Feldhake
#4 LOVE'S LATE SPRING, Lydia Heermann
#5 IN COMES LOVE, Mab Graff Hoover
#6 FOUNTAIN OF LOVE, Velma S. Daniels
      and Peggy E. King.
#7 MORNING SONG, Linda Herring
#8 A MOUNTAIN TO STAND STRONG,
      Peggy Darty
#9 LOVE'S PERFECT IMAGE, Judy Baer
#10 SMOKY MOUNTAIN SUNRISE,
      Yvonne Lehman
#11 GREENGOLD AUTUMN,
      Donna Fletcher Crow
#12 IRRESISTIBLE LOVE,
      Elaine Anne McAvoy
#13 ETERNAL FLAME, Lurlene McDaniel
#14 WINDSONG, Linda Herring
#15 FOREVER EDEN, Barbara Bennett
#16 THE DESIRES OF YOUR HEART,
      Donna Fletcher Crow
#17 CALL OF THE DOVE, Madge Harrah
#18 TENDER ADVERSARY, Judy Baer
#19 WAIT FOR THE SUN, Maryn Langer
#20 HOLD FAST THE DREAM,
      Lurlene McDaniel
#21 THE DISGUISE OF LOVE,
      Mary LaPietra

Serenade Saga Books are inspirational romances in historical settings, designed to bring you a joyful, heart-lifting reading experience.

Serenade Saga books available in your local bookstore:

#1 SUMMER SNOW, Sandy Dengler
#2 CALL HER BLESSED, Jeanette Gilge
#3 INA, Karen Baker Kletzing
#4 JULIANA OF CLOVER HILL,
     Brenda Knight Graham
#5 SONG OF THE NEREIDS, Sandy Dengler
#6 ANNA'S ROCKING CHAIR, Elaine Watson
#7 IN LOVE'S OWN TIME,
     Susan C. Feldhake
#8 YANKEE BRIDE, Jane Peart
#9 LIGHT OF MY HEART,
     Kathleen Karr
#10 LOVE BEYOND SURRENDER,
     Susan C. Feldhake
#11 ALL THE DAYS AFTER SUNDAY,
     Jeanette Gilge
#12 WINTERSPRING, Sandy Dengler
#13 HAND ME DOWN THE DAWN,
     Mary Harwell Sayler
#14 REBEL BRIDE, Jane Peart
#15 SPEAK SOFTLY, LOVE, Kathleen Yapp
#16 FROM THIS DAY FORWARD, Kathleen Karr
#17 THE RIVER BETWEEN, Jacquelyn Cook
#18 VALIANT BRIDE, Jane Peart
#19 WAIT FOR THE SUN, Maryn Langer
#20 KINCAID OF CRIPPLE CREEK,
     Peggy Darty
#21 LOVE'S GENTLE JOURNEY,
     Kay Cornelius